Shadows of Fathers

Simon Culleton

Stairwell Books //

Published by Stairwell Books
161 Lowther Street
York, YO31 7LZ

www.stairwellbooks.co.uk
@stairwellbooks

This is a work of fiction. Names, characters, businesses, places, events, locales, and incidents are either the products of the author's imagination or used in a fictitious manner. Any resemblance to actual persons, living or dead, or actual events is purely coincidental.

Cover art: Candy Joyce
Layout: Alan Gillott

ISBN: 978-1-913432-31-7
P8

To Florence and Joshua

Chapter 1

Autumn 1996

I DIDN'T EXPECT OTTO LEHMANN to be bald; it wasn't what I had imagined when crying to him on the phone from England. This was the man who said he could save everything so I assumed he would have a raging head of hair, like a lion.

As I opened the door to the reception area he walked across the spotless white tiled floor to meet me, running his hand over his shiny head. I strained not to look up at his baldness and he appeared to be concentrating not to focus on the red blotch on the side of my face. Our eyes met. We shook hands, he adding a second hand to make it less formal.

'You are late,' he said. *I'm drunk*, I thought.

'It's a miracle I've made it. My flight was the last one to land at Hamburg International airport yesterday evening.' Once at the hotel I had drained many bottles of Weiss beer and fell asleep on the floor, the side of my face pressed against the hot radiator.

He showed me into his office and gestured towards a polished leather swivel chair, which I gladly took, keeping both feet firmly on the ground.

'So Herr Archer,' he began while settling behind a dark mahogany desk, 'you want to see your children?'

'I want to take them back to England.'

1

He smiled, then frowned. 'I know this judge,' he said thoughtfully. 'I have, as we say in Germany, A brick in her wall. She will let you see your children, but to England, I think not.'

I tapped the envelope in my trouser pocket in which there was the means to have my children returned, but I had been strictly warned that at the risk of rendering it useless, not to present it until precisely the correct moment. Otto Lehmann glanced up to a clock on the wall. 'We have a little time,' he said, and pressed a button on his desk.

A timid secretary, whose auburn hair was tied in a neat bun, tiptoed in and offered coffee. We shared a smile as I declined the sugar. My gaze followed her as she left the room.

'She is beautiful person,' Herr Lehmann said. 'It is always good to have beauty around you, but sometimes the price is very high.'

I gave a quirky uncomprehending smile as I sipped my coffee.

'Your wife is beautiful, is she not?'

'You know her?'

'This is a small town, everybody knows everybody. Her father owns the tobacconist where I buy my newspapers every morning on my way to work. On the way home I will collect my order from the butchers next door to the tobacconist and maybe have a drink in the bar, which is next to that. Everybody knows everybody. Perhaps we should have a drink…or maybe not there, not yet.'

He ran his hand over his head once more, then stood up and peered out of the first floor view over the town centre. He noticed something and quickly beckoned me to join him. 'Quick bitte, come.'

I snapped to attention and was soon by his side and following his pointing finger. My heart almost stopped. Across the tree-lined square I recognized a yellow dress the colour of daffodils. I had bought her that dress two years previously. It was on a shopping trip in London; she had stepped out of the changing room cubical and whirled in front of me like a teenager.

She now hurried across the square, her blonde hair flailing behind her as she scurried in and out of the shadows cast by trees; a suited man, clutching some papers to his chest, followed her. His awkward stride was shorter than hers so that he continually broke into a trot to keep up.

'She's early,' I said.

'She's on time,' answered Herr Lehmann, then added without sarcasm, 'She's German.'

The two were soon out of view as they walked underneath the black and white canopy of the coffee shop underneath the office; but not before the suited man had briefly glanced up to our window. 'Ah, Herr Bauer,' muttered Herr Lehmann, with a respectful nod.

I walked back to my seat not knowing whether my hangover or the situation was causing the room to spin. A voice came from within the dark-grained mahogany desk and Herr Lehmann hurried over and answered with a flat passionless tone while holding down a button. He then looked up at me. 'Your wife and Herr Bauer are just being shown into the consultation room.'

Herr Lehmann then settled back into his seat resting his hands on the desk. His facial expression was kind and easy with a gentle gaze that asked no questions. For the first time I could link the man sitting in front of me to the one who I had sobbed to in desperation when telephoning from England. He used the same pacifying tone, which calmed me then, and now.

'Don't be worried Herr Archer, this is a good day. They are in the consultation room so they wish to negotiate. That is good. We can work on our differences and as you say in England, to iron them out before we go to the judge.'

'I want to take my children home,' I stated flatly. Herr Lehmann shook his head slowly and said, 'We are lucky that your wife chose Herr Bauer. He's a good colleague of mine and we always work well with each other and try to get our clients to talk.'

'Oh really,' I replied with fake surprise. 'Strange that he didn't recommend you when I accidentally phoned him first.' I instantly regretted my sharp comment.

Herr Lehmann ran a hand across his head once more and stood up. He forced a smile though was visibly taken aback by the comment.

'It is best we do not keep them waiting. It will not look good to the judge if we do not try to negotiate.'

'I don't want to negotiate,' I stated firmly.

Herr Lehmann walked over to the door and reached out to open it. I quickly rose from my seat and handed him the envelope. It was warm from being pressed against my leg in my trouser pocket and awkwardly creased. I quickly withdrew it and flattened it out on my chest before handing it back.

'What is this?' he asked.

'You see, I simply cannot negotiate,' I repeated.

Herr Lehmann walked back behind his desk, and reaching for a pair of small spectacles from his inside pocket, sat down and read in silence. After he had finished, and without looking up at me he picked up one of two telephones on his desk and tapped out a number.

My heart was thumping: I felt like a schoolboy in front of the head master, dizzy and frightened. He spoke in sharp official German, meaningless to my uncomprehending ears. I was acutely aware of his facial expression, his frown, his creased forehead, that he looked at me on certain sentences and away on others, his eyes widened when listening to the reply. My children's names were mentioned and I sat up.

4

Herr Lehmann replaced the telephone receiver and began to read the letter once more before looking up and staring in awkward silence. His eyes burned into the back of my head, a habit that in the many years of friendship to come, I would never quite get used to. A hint of a smile grew across his face as the cogs of his mind turned.

'You must have known that had I been aware of this letter before now I would have been legally obliged to inform Herr Bauer, who then surely would not have turned up today so as to avoid its ruling.' He raised his eyebrows and added, 'That's what I would have advised.'

'I told you I cannot negotiate, Herr Lehmann,' I repeated.

He was noticeably impressed and seemed to have a moment of deep thought before speaking.

'Put your elbows on the table,' he asked. I was stunned by the command. He repeated it in a softer tone and although I was openly confused I did as he asked. He then leaned across the table pushed my elbows and wrists together causing my forearms to form, all be it uncomfortably, a kind of elongated letter Y with my hands splayed out in either direction. His physical touch felt uncomfortable; I withdrew before being persuaded back into the same position again.

'I lived with the Sioux Indians,' he began.

Did he really say 'The Sioux Indians'?

'And they taught me,' he continued, 'to make this sign every time that I came to a fork in the road.'

As he spoke he ran his finger up the line of squashed flesh from my elbows to my wrists, stopping where my hands parted.

'This is your life-line and you have come to a fork in the road, you cannot go forward. Your old life is over and it is not for the spilt milk to be crying.'

'Can I take my arms down now?' I asked, but Herr Lehmann continued, 'You can either go this way.' Following the line of one of my hands, he added, 'and fight for your children. Or you can go the other way and let them go. You are still young; enjoy your life, your children will come back to you.' Then looking for a reaction, he added, 'Mine did.'

My eyes began to mist over and I swallowed hard.

'Did you lose your children to another country, another language?' Herr Lehmann looked towards the crumpled letter, which now lay discarded on the desk.

'That letter may help you with your children today but it is a sword with more than one edge. The judge will not be happy with the court procedure being stopped and if it does not work,' he now theatrically shrugged his shoulders, 'And if it doesn't work, it will make it harder for you to negotiate afterwards. You can put your arms down now.'

For the first time in our meeting my voice became harsh and sour although my anger was more to conceal the growing urge to sob.

'I just want to take my children back home.'

Herr Lehmann picked up the letter and walked towards the door again patting me on the shoulder as he passed. 'I would normally get my secretary to do this, but I think this time I shall tell Herr Bauer myself that he and his client cannot negotiate today.'

He disappeared out of the room, closing the door behind him. Then within a moment his shiny head reappeared. 'Who did Herr Bauer recommend for you?'

'Frau Fosher or Fisher.'

'Arrh Frau Fisher,' he repeated with a dismissive tone. 'Yes, he would prefer to have her against him than me.' Before disappearing again he looked at me with a warm smile. 'This is a good day, Herr Archer, because it is me that you have.'

Chapter 2

Three weeks earlier

EVA SAT IN THE PASSENGER seat with her grey blue eyes fixed on the road ahead, the flight tickets clutched in her hands. The children were in the back, sleeping in their car seats, their heads swaying to the motion. We mostly remained silent until the road sign to the airport came into view, which prompted Eva into conversation.

She spoke of trivial things, the garden fence; the curtains in the front room, things that she would change or fix on her return; things, I thought later, to reassure me that she was coming back.

'I'm happy with the curtains in the front room,' I said, 'but change them if you like.'

'They are not actually our curtains, Hanna loaned them to us,' she said while peering into the vanity mirror and running a brush through her hair.

I feigned surprise.

'Hanna has no curtains in her front room so that we can have some?'

Eva frowned. 'They are her spare pair, but please Richard, I promised you would return them while I was gone. Be nice to her, she is the only German friend I have in England.'

I gave a dismissive huff.

'She always speaks in German to you in front of me. She knows I don't understand.'

'You have never truly bothered to learn to speak German. No one in this country ever does.' There was a short silence.

'I'll compromise. I'll take half the curtains back.' Eva continued to stare at the road ahead.

'You're not funny. Everybody in this country thinks they're so funny.'

Eva hurriedly searched in her handbag before reaching back to Louise and wiping the side of her dribbling mouth with a tissue.

The twinkling lights of the airport terminal appeared on the horizon. I was soon searching for a space in the thirty minute car park. We held a child each and walked through a long concrete underpass to the departure terminal, our footsteps echoing. We entered through the sliding doors and were immediately engulfed in a sea of people.

At the security gate I stopped to hug my children goodbye. They looked pitiful and tired standing there, not fully awake from the sleep in the car. Both Louise, our four-year-old girl and Sebastian, our five-year-old boy still smelt of their beds. Their coats were zipped up and they reminded me of wartime evacuees; about to be sent to the countryside. I knelt down to Louise and she stretched her arms around my neck and then Sebastian, who seemed more aware of the situation, joined in the group hug. I told them Daddy loved them. 'It's only for a week,' I said, holding their heads close to mine. 'Then you will be back home again.'

Eva rolled her eyes. 'Don't make a scene, Richard.'

My hug with Eva was quick, like awkward distant cousins at a wedding; a kind of prolonged pat-on-the-back; although for a split second, right at the very end, our embrace was tight. Eva was eager to be gone. I watched until their faces disappeared in the crowd and I felt as if I had been punched in the stomach.

9

I DROVE BACK TO MY hometown of Chelmsford stopping off at a large store along the way. Soon I was walking up the path to my home carrying a plastic bag full of apples, chocolate, a bottle of wine and a lasagne with cooking instructions that assured me that it would be ready to serve to my family in four microwave minutes. I fumbled in the darkness with my keys then pushed a pile of free newspapers and junk mail as I opened the front door. The front-room curtains had not been drawn and the streetlights shone in casting unfamiliar shadows across the furniture. I walked from room to room switching on all the lights. The house was hauntingly still and in the same, hurriedly left state from that morning; cupboards doors open, clothes hanging out of drawers, like a crime scene

*

WITHIN TWO NIGHTS OF SLEEPING alone I had drifted to the middle of the bed, curling the covers up around my chin and tucking them under my thighs leaving no space for sharing. I had yet to eat seated at the table in the kitchen. I opted instead for the single armchair in the living room in front of the television, balancing a plate on my knees and watched re-runs of black and white war films where the Germans were always terrible shots.

Eva had not phoned to say they had made it safely to Germany, something she would have normally done. I was eager to hear from her and had already twice lunged across the furniture to pick up the phone only to hear a call about work. I was reluctant to be the first to call; I wanted to be the one that was needed. I had suspected or rather hoped that a busy family agenda had prevented her from calling. The children would have been pre-occupied by their Grandparents who allowed them down from the upstairs apartment to run around the tobacconist shop during opening hours.

Come the third day I arrived home early from work and relented. I picked up the phone receiver before I had even taken my coat off. The call went straight through to the shop and Eva's mother, 'the wicked witch of the North', took the call. She, no doubt would be sitting behind the shop counter, smoking a cigarette and tapping ash into an over-flowing, ruby red *Marlboro* ashtray.

'Can I speak to Eva,' I said in clear, well-spaced English words knowing that Eva's mother, like myself, knew little of other languages. She coughed before she spoke then said something in sharp German, which I didn't understand. Normally there would have been some humble attempt to use English where a few memorized phrases like, '*Not here,*' or '*later call bitte*' would be gratefully received. This time it was all in German and I noted with my limited knowledge that I had gained from a few night classes that she ended the sentence with the formal and somewhat old fashion '*Auf wiederhörten*' as opposed to the friendly '*Tschüss*' for 'goodbye'. Then the line went dead. Although my first thought was to bite the receiver in two, I could at least console myself that a message would be passed on to Eva and the children that Daddy had called.

On the fourth day I sat down at the kitchen table to read some of the accumulated mail, avoiding the envelopes marked *electric* or *gas*, that for now would be add to the growing pile stacked behind the sugar pots of bills yet unpaid.

An invitation to the school reunion, wrapped in a gold sleeve, had momentarily lifted my spirits. A flash of memory, sitting in the classroom, the smell of cut grass wafting through the window, Helen Saunders two rows forward, flicking her hair behind her ear. I resolved then and there not to go.

As I fanned the letters across the table I recognized the red Deutsche post stamp. I was perplexed but not overly worried.

11

Perhaps Eva, I hoped, had helped the children write me a loving letter saying they missed me.

I carefully took a butter knife, ripped open the seal and laid its contents in front of me. It was a typed letter on stiff, crisp watermarked paper, which was finished with a swirling hand-written signature. Apart from my name and address, I could comprehend little of it. So I scampered to the bookshelf in the front room to find the German/English dictionary.

I returned to the kitchen and cleared space on the table where I now placed the dictionary open besides the letter. I began to decipher its contents but soon became entrenched.

The German language, as I was rapidly learning, is particular in adding words onto other words to make another word, which can then be staggeringly long and completely different from the original word that one started with. So when referencing a single word, it is possible to have five deviations that could replace it. It was frustrating work. Understanding some of the smaller words: unt, sie es ist, were of little use if I didn't comprehend the longer words. The Germans, as it seems, do love a long word.

After an hour of scrutinizing and finger-licking page turning I had only three words translated to an acceptable degree: I had written them on a pad next to the letter: *Unfortunate, regrettable, legislation.* These words were still not enough to get the true sense of the contents until with the next word, like a pivotal piece in a jigsaw puzzle, the face of a grandfather clock or the number on a gate post, did the letter slowly revealed itself.

I had the letters of *s c h e i*, which I gradually accumulated as I ran my finger down the page of the dictionary until I found the next needed letter of d and read the word next to it: *Scheide:* which translated to *vagina.*

'My God,' I thought and checked again to see that the letter was addressed to me before carrying on. Then half way down the second page I found the full word: Scheidung. *Divorce.*

I sat back in my chair, staring at my translated words written on the pad. Like the dampness that precedes rain, I had felt this coming for weeks, especially in the days leading up to the holiday. Also, in the car on the journey to the airport when we spoke about the things that we would do when she returned. We had been playing happy family for weeks. It wasn't the arguments; it was the lack of them.

Five years previously she arrived in England pregnant and happy to be away from dismissive family frowns at her, then, unmarried statue. England was the promise land. Yet now her blue suitcase under the bed seemed permanently filled with the folded squares of children's clothes. Always another trip home to Germany.

I didn't question the heavy suitcase this time as I carried it to the car. I just thought it was packed with presents for her family.

I looked back at the letter. I still had a paragraph to go, in particular a sentence that was printed in bold text followed by the names of my children. It took another hour to understand it: Das Sorgerecht behalten: I had two translated choices: *Keep the care* or *Retain the custody.*

Chapter 3

I ARRIVED AT THE BUSINESS premises of P.J. Smith, an office supply company that also translated foreign language texts. A line of soapy water underneath the large business name painted onto the window showed the window cleaner had just been by.

On the short walk from my house to the stone bridge in the middle of my hometown, everything looked different today. Mr Patel's corner shop with its flaky paint work, the crumbling old red brick wall weakened by ivy on one street corner, the leaning apple tree that reached over the path at another and the neat, manicured front garden where once I'd seen an old lady with dementia trying to mow her front lawn with a vacuum cleaner; it all looked different today because my world had changed, so everything had changed. I felt like a foreigner seeing it all for the first time, a feeling I would soon experience with added realism in the German town of Ahrensburg.

I took the letter out of my jean pocket and flatten it upon the gleaming white reception desk. I had hastily scribbled notes in the margins and underlined many words, yet thankfully it was still decipherable. I rang a silver bell which was next to a sign that asked me to wait. A single ding hung in the air. I watched the movement of blurred outlines through the smoked glass of the office door behind the counter. A clean-cut man wearing a blue shirt opened the door. Behind him I could see several women wearing headsets, sitting at their desks, rhythmically typing. I showed him the letter, which he immediately acknowledged it as being written in German although he confessed he did not read it himself.

'French is my bag,' he said, then beckoned a woman from her desk. She was rather young, not long out of university, I presumed. She spoke in a foreign accent that I did not recognise as German.

'There are some very long legal words here,' she said while reading. 'The Germans like their long words.'

'You're telling me,' I said.

'I will have to look them up,' she continued. 'When has this got to be translated by?'

'Can't you just tell me now?' I asked. 'It's very important. It's about my...' I hesitated to use the word divorce. 'Well, you can work that out yourself,' I continued. The young woman looked over to the man in the blue shirt who had remained within earshot. He reached under the counter and produced a price list which I read with disbelieving eyes.

'£50 for one page!' I exclaimed. The student gave me a pitying smile. I felt ashamed at my ignorance and quickly leafed through my wallet for the cash. They agreed to send it out by express delivery as soon as it was finished.

Moments later I stepped outside, feeling somewhat dazed at having handed over almost a day's wages in one transaction. I continued to walk along the high street looking for somewhere to sit and contemplate my next move. Eventually I found an empty bench next to an over flowing rubbish bin. The remains of a pushbike had been chained to the bench; its wheels and saddle had already been stolen. It looked like the skeleton of an animal that had been left to starve. I perched on the end of the bench rubbing my hands.

A mother with a pushchair walked past me and I looked in the face of the child for my own children. I wished I had taken the time to learn German and felt a lesser father for not being able to read the words in the letter about them.

I had, of course, travelled to Germany and tried to speak the language, but the locals, being kind people and generous hosts, would always take the opportunity to practice their own English. I eagerly obliged.

Suddenly in the distance I heard a shriek, a child's familiar scream and I felt certain I had heard the word 'Daddy'. My heart missed a beat and I stood up and instinctively ran towards the two familiar little figures that were holding hands accompanied by an adult. An unexpected feeling of glee powered my legs as a dozen questions filled my head... How, when, who cares? Relief gushed from my body like an evil spirit exorcised. I opened my arms to receive them. The children stopped in their tracks and the mother, who at first looked to recognize me, pulled the children aside to let me pass. I stopped short of colliding with them and for the first time focused on their unfamiliar faces and not the matching red parka jackets with the fur lined hoods, identical to the ones I had recently noted were no longer hanging on the coat hooks by the front door.

'Sorry,' I pleaded, 'please forgive me, I thought they were...' The mother passed, keeping herself between her children and me. I watched the children's little bodies waddle off in their oversized coats, like penguins. My knees wobbled with the sudden loss of spirit. I felt the immediate need to hold my children, to see my family, hear them. I ran for home speeding past the pushchair mother and her baby again, back over the stone bridge. I ran and jogged and caught my breath and stopped to rest against the ivy-covered wall. The local postman noticed me from the other side of the road. Had he caught me, he would have rambled on about his exotic fish. I pretended I didn't see him and jogged off again. I arrived at my door panting like an over-heated dog and pushed in the key. I rushed to phone and held the receiver to my ear, listening to the long continuous tone. I was at first unable to dial. Eva would know by now that I had received the letter.

I tapped out the number, the long seconds between each buzz. I was a schoolboy again, sweaty palms, knee joints not entirely steady. Then I heard the voice of Eva and I felt relieved and nervous at the same time. She answered in swift, rolling German. I imagined her to be standing up. I waited for a few polite seconds afterwards before saying quietly, 'It's me.' Silence followed, so I spoke again. 'I got your letter.'

More long drawn out seconds before Eva eventually spoke.

'Then you know.'

'I don't know exactly,' I snarled, 'the letter's in German.'

There was a sigh before Eva began to speak in a tone not entirely familiar; it was cordial and pacifying, the way a parent might speak to a teenager. Her words seemed calculated, her phrases rehearsed. Her one small fault was that she spoke a little fast, which was the only hint that she was nervous too. I tried to interrupt, wait for a pause to ask a question but she was in control and this was not a question and answer session. So I listened as the beats in my chest increased. I knew what was coming around the corner.

'It isn't just you,' she said, 'it is everything: it's the country, the house, the food, the television. I can't understand some of the accents; and the weather, yes the silly weather, it never snows. I grew up with snow,' she pleaded. 'And, and,' she began to stutter, 'your stupid British humour. Everyone in England thinks they are so funny. How many times must I hear jokes about England beating Germany in the war?'

17

'Two wars,' I stated, then instantly regretted having said it. In the silence that followed I could visualize Eva rolling her eyes. Eventually she spoke. 'I'm not coming back.'

'Don't be silly.'

'I mean it. I'm not coming back.'

'Is there somebody else?' My heart beat increased.

'Why must there be somebody else?'

'There is always somebody else.'

'There is nobody else. It's the country. I can't live there anymore.'

'Eva,' I wanted to say, 'I love' but my voice wobbled. We were finally having *that* conversation. Eva's tone became sharper. 'I'm not coming back. Read the letter.'

I didn't want to talk about the letter, about my hours of translating and the awful words on the pad.

'Come back, Eva. We can't do this on the phone.' There was another short silence.

'Richard, I want a divorce.'

It took a moment for me to answer. 'Well, come back and we can sort it out.'

'I'm divorcing you from here.'

I swallowed hard. My voice wobbled again and I began muttering.

'My God,' I said, 'you're not bringing the children back.'

Then I began to speak quickly, my words bursting from my mouth; begging mutterings that soon turned into frantic pleas. I became pathetic, undignified. I exhausted my breath while pleading for her to come home, to bring my family home. I waited in silence for a reply only to realize that the phone line was dead. She had long since gone.

I was walking the streets some time later in the early morning, so early in fact that the birds had yet to awaken. A dull gloom was slowly lifting. I found myself outside Sebastian's infant school although I couldn't recall deciding to head for it. No less than two months previously I had walked Sebastian to his allotted classroom for his first day at school. Now, across the playground, his classroom looked cold and sad, like an empty cinema.

I climbed over the gates easily and walked across the playground, my footsteps making the only sound. At the foot of the classroom were two wooden steps, which led to the door. When I put my weight upon the top step, it creaked loudly. I froze at the sudden noise. The door was half glass with posters stuck on the inside. I found a gap and stared through. One of the items that Sebastian had received in his first day welcome-pack was a name-tag that he could hang on his own chosen coat hook. All of the parents were allowed into the classroom to help their children settle in. I had selected Sebastian's coat hook for him; third from the right; and allowed him to hook his own coat on. Now Sebastian's name tag was nowhere to be seen.

Chapter 4

'IT IS OBVIOUSLY AN INTERNATIONAL matter,' I was assured by a sharply dressed advisor at the Citizen's Advice Bureau. He was wearing an expensive three-piece suit that I found profoundly inappropriate amongst the tracksuit-wearing participants in the waiting room. I thought upon his words for a moment as I sat in a small cubical, my back facing the listening people who sat waiting for their number to be called.

'International, that sounds serious,' I mused and he agreed with a raised eyebrow. 'Expensive too,' he added.

'What if I just go to Germany grab my children and bring them back?'

He leaned back in his chair and spoke in a more earnest fashion.

'It is quite possible,' he said, 'that you may be prosecuted under Germany law for child abduction.'

My reply was loud enough to quieten the muttering audience. 'How can I abduct my own children?'

The suited advisor remained unfazed. His gold chain slipped down his wrist as he leaned across the table, drawing closer to me.

'It doesn't mean that you are helpless,' he continued. 'It just means that it's a matter of international law. The English courts have no jurisdiction over the German courts and the German courts have no jurisdiction over our English courts, not unless it's an international law that both countries have signed up to.' He stared at me until I nodded before continuing.

'It would be different if the children were still in the country, then we could have possibly stopped them from leaving.' I sighed heavily and the adviser quickly moved on.

'Are your wife and children likely to return?' he asked. I shook my head.

'Why should she?' He motioned me to wait while he went off to consult with another member of staff. I sat patiently and listened to the other conversations that were now buzzing in the neighbouring cubicles.

'I've ran out of gas to heat the house,' said one woman, who then elaborated by stating that she had to cuddle up to her cat to keep warm. There was a young lad on the other side of me who was continually sniffing and referred to the advisor as Bruv: 'I ain't got nowhere to sleep Bruv, except me mate's sofa. It ain't right Bruv, it ain't right Bruv, you know what I mean Bruv.'

These were valid and sincere requests on any other day, no matter how unrefined they may have been presented; but today, I was contemplating losing my children and I wanted to scream it to the ceiling and tear down the dividing cubicle to tell them so.

My advisor returned with a raised eyebrow and a slightly smug smile. He slid a piece of paper across the counter with a name and address written on it. He pointed at the name as he spoke. 'And don't forget to say you voted for him even if you didn't.'

The advisor then shook my hand firmly making me feel sufficiently important. He promised to contact me if he found any addition information and that he would phone ahead now to book an emergency appointment.

He finished by handing me a bundle of leaflets and booklets of organizations that I was now eligible to join before showing me the door. I briefly flicked through the titles as I walked to my next destination: *Crises in the family, Relate, Living with depression, Suicide is never the answer.* 'Blimey,' I thought.

I was fortunate that the M.P.'s surgeries, which were held twice weekly, were taking place on that particular day. Strange that with all of the doom and gloom that hung around me like fog I actually felt excited to be there.

The M.P.'s address was in a normal suburban road where a downstairs room of a traditional Georgian house had been converted to receive constituents. I had rarely been in the company of a politician. Of course I had seen them on the television in the 'House of Commons' and occasionally a politician would knock on my door during election time. They wore big rosettes pinned to their lapels, which reminded me of a clown's hidden water pistol. They had always seemed a different breed of person, stiff and formal, whose passion were controlled by five syllable words and historical references. A purposeful ploy to confuse, I had always thought.

My elected M.P. was the right honourable Simon Steed, Member of Parliament for the Conservative Party. A secretary, perched behind a small antique writing desk looked over the rims of her half-cup glasses as I entered. She asked me to be seated on one of two brown chesterfield sofas. Then she silently arose and glided across the oak herringbone floor to a large door and gently tapped twice before slipping inside. Within moments she reappeared stating in a loud whisper that Simon Steed was ready to receive me.

Mr Steed sat low behind a bulky desk that was covered in smooth green leather. He was reading a document as I entered and I wondered if he had just picked it up to pretend to be busy, because that's what I would have done. A large portrait of Margret Thatcher hung above a fireplace, her eyes bearing down on me. Mr Steed, it seemed, made no attempt to look anything other than a politician, with his double-breasted navy pinstripe suit jacket, cufflinks and a gold clip held mid-way down his conservative crested blue tie. I would not have been surprised had he offered me a cigar and brandy, though he did not. We shook hands firmly although Mr Steed did not rise from his seat to do so.

'So Mr Archer,' he began, 'our colleagues from the Citizens Advice Bureau have phoned ahead to say that you are having a little problem with your marriage.' I immediately burst into conversation, like a waterfall of information; someone was listening, someone wanted to know! I could have hugged him although I fear he may have resented the crumpling of his suit.

'It's not my marriage, it's the children. Well it is the marriage but it's about the children.' I was already beginning to stutter my words. 'She's taken the children to Germany or rather she's not bringing them back. No one has the right to take my children away, surely. I miss them, I, I…think of them all of the time…I, I.'

My mouth became dry as I gasped for the words that would not come. I fell into an awkward silence. Yet Simon Steed did not interrupt. His facial expression had remained genuine and sincere. For all of his showy contrived appearance, which gave off the opinion of cold detachment, Mr Steed had the courtesy and professionalism to know I had more to say. 'It's not right, is it?' I continued, 'my children were born here; no-one has the right to take them away. It's not right?' I almost ended with the word *Bruv* like the lad in the cubical.

Simon Steed took his eyes away from me for a brief moment while he wrote on the piece of paper. In the silence that ensued I strained to read his spider handwriting.

'Is your wife German?' he asked

'Completely,' I answered. Simon Steed thought for a moment then began, 'Let us just say there is a wife who is not very happy.'

'She was never happy,' I interrupted. Mr Steed blinked slowly in irritation.

'Let's us just say,' he repeated, 'that there is a wife, not your wife but any wife, and she is not very happy living in this country.' I went along with his non-committal third person analogy. 'So this wife being not very happy with her lot, takes the children to another country, perhaps the country of her birth, and makes up loads of reasons of why she cannot return. Is this sounding familiar?'

I nodded.

'Let us go further,' he continued, 'to say that the father wants them back which is against the mother's wishes.'

I sat up, happy that I had now entered the story.

'This now becomes a matter of international law if indeed an international law has been broken.'

He then looked at me accusingly and my cheeks reddened.

'Did you ever?' he asked, 'Did you ever agree or make any form of agreement with your wife for the children to stay in Germany permanently?' I was rather taken aback by his directness.

'No, no, I thought they were going on holiday.' I didn't mention my suspicions of the weeks leading up to the day they left, of the arguments that suddenly stopped, of the heavy suitcase that I'd loaded into the car boot before driving them to the airport.

Mr Steed relaxed in his seat, his speech was over. There was a sudden knock at the door and the spectacle-wearing secretary popped her head around in what I presumed to be a prearranged interruption to reminded visitors not to over stay their welcome.

'Your next appointment has arrived,' she said. 'Mr Steed acknowledged her with a nod of his head then began writing again while talking to me.

'I'm going to speak to some of our people in Parliament,' he said.

'Parliament. That sounds serious.' He finished writing before he answered. 'It is serious. You should get a letter in a couple of days.'

'A letter.' I tried to smile as I spoke but was openly deflated. Mr Steed could see the enthusiasm drain from my face.

'Chin up,' he said, 'never underestimate the power of the pen.'

The secretary appeared once more at the doorway and remained holding it open. I took the hint and after his firm impressive handshake in which his hand felt warm, I rose from my seat to leave. I couldn't help but look up to the imposing portrait of Margret Thatcher who had been staring down at me throughout the meeting.

'She would never stand for it,' I said.

Simon Steed answered without looking up from the papers he was now reading. 'Margret Thatcher,' he said, 'would have never married a German.'

I WALKED HOME WITH THE Autumn sun on my face. I felt uplifted by the meeting with Mr Simon Steed and wanted to share it with my children.

Once again I listened to the distinctive passionless one-note hum of the German ring tone, which increased my apprehension. It was late afternoon, the tobacconist shop would still be open and the call would go directly through to the shop counter. This would annoy Eva's parents' routine but I didn't care.

Within two rings the receiver was sharply picked up and the voice of Eva's mother answered in a flat tone. I spoke in slow clear English.

'I want to speak to my children.' There was no answer except a clunking sound, which I presumed was the receiver being put down on a hard surface. I could hear muttering in the background, an unfamiliar voice, which I guessed by its inflexion to be a customer. Then as if to confirm this I heard the opening of a cash register. It was the end of the day and the people of Ahrensburg, on their way home from work would be hurrying into the shop to replace their dwindling supply of pipe tobacco or a box of five cigars. Newspapers were also sold and the newly introduced 'lotto' ticket machine had been installed. The tobacconist was situated between a butcher's shop and a small bar with tall outside tables, ensuring a steady stream of customers.

The phone receiver would have to be picked up in the upstairs apartment before it could be disconnected in the shop. I heard a distant calling of my children's names, which made me catch my breath. Then there was a click and the noise from the shop ceased. There was silence but for the sound of gentle breathing. I waited for a moment.

'It's me,' I said softly, 'Daddy.' Still more silence.

'Who is this?' I continued in my gentle tone. I could still hear the breathing of a single person, or was it two?

'I miss you so much. Please somebody talk to me. It's Daddy. I love you.'

'Where are you Daddy?' came the reply. I burst into floods of relief.

'Oh my little girl, my little darling, I miss you, I miss you.'

Sebastian's voice now spoke too. 'I've got a new Superman.'

'It's my lovely boy too,' I said with heightened surprise. I realised that they must have been holding the phone together. 'Oh I miss you, I miss you both.'

I ignored the fact that Sebastian had spoken the word *super* in the German fashion pronouncing the s as z for: *zuperman.*

'And Postman Pat, where is Postman Pat?' Sebastian had watched the Postman Pat videos relentlessly and carried a figurine around with him everywhere, tucking it under the covers at bedtime.

There was an awkward silence before Louise stated, 'He's lost it.' I was quick to tell him not to worry, that I would buy another; I would buy them both a present. I continued in this fashion; speaking to them then listening to their replies, pressing the receiver to my ear, capturing every sound in my head like it was pure nectar. Yet sometimes the conversation staggered. Up until now I had not contemplated how difficult it would be to converse at length with a four and a five-year-old even if they were my own, especially on the phone. This would be a side to parenting that I had yet to learn and for my first attempt I was doing terribly. I spoke about the sunny day and the leaves falling from the trees and the squirrels that hopped from branch to branch. Yet I was running out of ideas.

'Are you still there?' I asked and thankfully they both replied with a simple 'yes'.

'Where is your mother?' I couldn't help but ask.

'Oma is looking after us.' That was a generous version of the truth, as I knew her to be downstairs in the shop. I could almost smell the tobacco rising up the stairs and knew my children would be breathing in the stench from a tobacco-stained telephone receiver.

There was sudden dull thud and the children's voices became distant. They argued and it became apparent that the receiver had been dropped. I tried to tell them to be good, to pick up the phone. I pleaded for one of them to pick up. There was a scream and Louise began to cry. My clammy hand gripped the receiver tightly as if I was actually holding onto the children themselves. Helpless, helpless, I knocked the earpiece against my forehead.

'Please pick up.' I became desperate. 'Postman Pat, Postman Pat, Postman Pat and his black and white cat,' I started to sing. I knew the words by heart. I sang the whole thing aloud and waited for a response. I could hear muffled movements but it did not seem close. So I sang again, imagined my little voice coming from the phone receiving laying on the carpet at the top of the stairs. Eventually I drifted into silence unable to disconnect. I could just make out the sound of German cartoons coming from a television and was sure I could hear soft footsteps close by. A click, then a long passionless hum of a dial tone.

Chapter 5

THE FOLLOWING MORNING, I WAS up early, waiting outside of my house for my lift to work to arrive. I recalled with a shudder a time only a few months earlier when I had witnessed something that only now could I fully comprehend.

I was working late on a London building site, the same one, in fact that I was heading to today. The building site at that time was in the early stages of the construction of a large comprehensive school. Dark unlit concrete corridors yet to be painted in bright encouraging colours can be a gloomy, windy, almost haunting place when working alone. My only comfort had been a few distant voices to remind me that I was not the only one working late. I walked towards the human sound and began to fix plasterboard to the ceiling in the same room as one of the workmen. He nodded to me as I entered but continued his conversation with the other workmate even though a partition wall obscured their view of each other. Fortunately for their husky tobacco-scarred voices, the wall had yet to be installed with sound insulation. Both men admitted to enduring the shared doom of divorce which was, in part, the same reason why they were both working late. The solicitor's fees, child maintenance and cost of the now one-room bedsit were crippling and there was the original family mortgage still to pay. The pre-divorced days of working Saturday morning to cover the extra bills were a mere fanciful luxury of another era. They delved into each other's situation, not as two men competing for 'the best of the worst' but as reassurance that neither was alone in his suffering.

'I've got nothing left,' shouted one, 'she's taken the lot and now she won't let me see the children until I pay more.'

'Haven't seen mine for a three months. She's seen to that,' replied the other in a depressing confession. It was a distressing conversation for me to overhear although at the time I didn't know why.

'It's all about the money,' one of them repeated. 'Money, money, money and they use the children as a bargaining chip to get it.'

'Exactly,' agreed the other. They continued in that way, shouting through the wall, unable to see each other. They spoke of the empty nights of staring at the faded wallpaper in their smelly bedsit and the lack of sleep from the thumping bass from the social-security boys in the flat above; of take-away food balanced on their laps in front of a black and white portable televisions whereas three months previous they had sat with their families watching a 26-inch colour TV in their own front room. They could have been exaggerating, competing with ever-expanding stories as men often do. But I knew they were speaking their truth and it was precisely that which filled me with dread. I wanted to reject them and ignore their existence because I feared them as a race of men I was about to join. I had seen them everywhere, these shadows of men; almost fathers, wannabe dads, who lurked on the periphery of normal family life. Holding onto their fatherhood as the only reason for being. These shabbily dressed men in crumpled clothes; men with five-o-clock stubble who smoked continually at the school gates amongst crowds of tut-tutting mothers and waited in dread in case their children were embarrassed to see them; sitting in steamed-up cars in the car-parks of playing fields on rainy days where bored children drew pictures with their fingers in the condensation; fathers with empty stares who had lost their dignity. These shadow fathers, who could only come together through a partition wall so their drawn, creased facial expressions could be excluded from view, hidden from each other and concealed by a macho voice. These men were not only working late to gain the precious extra pounds that might enable them to see their children, which was reason enough to give to other men. But they were avoiding the truth no less than I was pretending not to recognise it…they were working late because they had nowhere else to go.

I suddenly heard the rumble of Dave's van and watched his faded blue Ford transit with trusty arches come into view. It sounded like a Lancaster bomber. He pulled up outside of my house and I was quick to get in before the neighbours were awoken. The smell of tobacco clogged my nostrils as I brushed back the old newspapers and crisp packets from the passenger seat to make space for me to sit.

'The seatbelt is broken,' I said as the van pulled away.

'I know,' replied Dave, whose ginger-bearded face barely showed the movement of his lips. 'Just hold it over your body in case the police see you.'

'But what about if we crash?'

'Seat belt won't save you,' he huffed. 'It's the brakes you want to worry about.' There was no sign of humour in his voice. I watched his oily hand grind the stick through the gears and felt sure that he had spent yet another weekend trying to fix an already dilapidated work van.

'How was your week off?' Dave asked as he lit a cigarette with both hands while steering with his knees. My blood pressure rose and I waited for him to take hold of the stirring wheel again before I answered.

'Ok!' I shouted over the roar of the engine. I felt thankful that he did not know that my wife and children had not returned from Germany. Also I hoped his question was more of a formality than an inquiry. I felt fortunate that the roar of a blown exhaust defied any real chance of conversation.

A sudden jerk of the vehicle and Dave swore as the van swerved violently. I looked into the rear view mirror to see a cyclist making rude hand gestures. Dave drove at break neck speed taking each corner like a toboggan. I did momentarily forget my depression and replace it with sheer terror. Eventually we arrived at the construction site with a feeling akin to a miner appearing out into the sunlight after another perilous shift down the pits.

'We made it on time again,' announced Dave as he switched the engine off, 'two seconds quicker than yesterday.' I released my white-knuckle grip from the broken seatbelt.

I soon began unpacking the plastering tools from the back of the van and walked with my heavy load to my place, to begin working on a wall. Bearded labourer Dave soon entered the room, pushing a wheelbarrow full of cement that he had mixed to such perfection he declared it good enough to eat.

In the van on the journey home Dave attempted to shout over the roar of the engine.

'So when does the wife and kids come back from Germany? I thought they were only going for a week.' I pretended not to have heard him so he repeated his question when we pulled up outside my home. We both looked towards my house; the curtains still undrawn as I had left then that morning.

I confessed.

'They are not coming back; she's keeping the children in Germany. My God, Dave I'm desperate.' His dust bitten eyes narrowed and a small frown was visible in-between his dangling fringe and bushy beard. I was touched by his genuine concern.

'What are you doing here, mate?' he asked. 'Why don't you just go to Germany and get them back? That's what I would do.'

I answered sharply. 'Do you think I haven't thought about it? But it's not as simple as that.'

There was a moment of silence before Dave spoke softly, 'What you need is a good English solicitor to get them back. Do you know any?'

'Yes Dave, I met one this morning by the cement mixer… Of course I don't. Besides I can't afford solicitors, I'm a plasterer and they wouldn't want the case anyway.'

'But it's free,' insisted Dave, who now spoke with enthusiasm. 'Well at least for the first half hour. It's this new promotion all of the solicitors are doing. First half an hour free, no win no fee, that sort of thing. They take any case. My mate wanted to sue his neighbour for running over his cat and they took the case.'

'Did he win?'

'No, it was the wrong cat. His own cat came home four days later so everyone's now trying to work out whose cat they buried but that's not the point, the solicitors still argued the case.'

I had to admit he was right. Dave, the plasterer's labourer, who had never aspired to improve his life any more than he did his van or his beard had inadvertently shamed me into action. I had little faith in M.P., the Right Honourable Simon Steed and his Parliamentary letter. Perhaps it was time for Daddy to take the lead.

*

I pushed through the glass doors of the solicitor's office, which opened into a crowded waiting room. Many faces turned to look at me. The reception desk was situated at the other end so I had to walk the gauntlet through outstretched legs and handbags. I whispered my details to the receptionist who then asked me to take a seat. A young acne-ridden male of about 16 years old moved over one seat to allow me to sit between him and a woman which I soon realised to be his mother. The boy wore a badly fitting supermarket suit and the woman's cheeks were powered so thickly that I could have scraped a phone number in them.

I briefly glanced around at the people in the waiting room: a young couple holding hands next to an old man biting his nails; a father and son with identically folded arms sat in silence next to a large lady in ski pants who surreptitiously dipped her hand into her handbag before bringing a crisp to her mouth. Most wore the same stricken, nervous facial expressions.

The woman leaned over me and spoke to the boy; her breath smelt of bacon and tea.

'Now remember Shane, sit up straight and call the man Sir, they like that kind of thing.'

'Yes Mum.'

'And don't forget to mention that you want the free 30 minutes consultation.'

'Yes Mum.' The boy shifted uncomfortably in his stiff nylon trousers.

Then another suited man appeared by the reception desk and called out a name. The boy next to me shot up to attention.

'I want the free 30 minutes please,' he said then prompted by his mother added, 'Sir'. The solicitor smiled professionally.

'Do follow me,' he said.

Then just as my mind began to wander and different people were called and other equally nervous people took their seats, I heard my name. I followed the backs of his shiny shoes. Once in his office he showed me to a seat then struggled to squeeze behind his desk. He was a large man dressed in an expensively tailored dark blue suit, which seemed a little tight. He fell into his seat with a huff. I quickly began.

'I'd like to take advantage of the free 30 minutes consultation please.'

He breathed out heavily. 'Certainly,' he said.

He then concentrated at the clock on the wall and waited for the second hand to reach twelve before speaking.

'So Mr Archer, I'm Mr Horsham. How may I help you?' His stare was surprisingly intense. I hesitated for a moment.

'My wife is divorcing me,' I spluttered, '…and we have two young children and I want custody.' Mr Horsham gave a wry smile.

'I see,' he began, 'Well, we don't call it that anymore. There is no such thing as custody.' I felt immediately uplifted.

'One parent,' he continued, 'has the full time parental control and the other has what is newly termed as *visitation rights*.' He emphasised the last two words.

'So, is that joint custody?' I asked. Mr Horsham shifted uncomfortably in his seat.

'No it's nothing like joint custody, which legally never really existed. You, the father, will get visitation rights.'

'I thought joint custody did exist,' I protested and searched my memory for an example. I could think of none. Mr Horsham confidently contradicted me.

'You are mistaken, Mr Archer.' Mr Horsham appeared to read the disappointment on my face. 'Respectfully I say that you probably know loads of parents where the mother agrees to share, but she has no legal obligation to do so. The legal arrangement of child sharing simply does not exist, I'm very sorry to say.'

'Why not?' I sounded desperate. Mr Horsham softened his tone.

'Say for instance, one of your children, God forbid were in desperate need of an operation that could dramatically improve the child's life, but the operation came with some risks. The mother was prepared to take the risk of an operation but the father was not. Somebody has to take the lead; you see my point?' I was caught off guard and could think of no answer at that moment.

'But you will get visitation rights,' he stated optimistically.

'How do you know?'

Mr Horsham gestured a hand towards me. 'Because you are the father.'

'And the mother gets the custody?' I added.

'Yes, the mother will get the parental control…custody, but we don't call it that anymore.'

'So what are the chances of me, the father getting "parental control"?' I said, sarcastically emphasising the phrase. Mr Horsham began to speak in a slower, more attentive tone, which I found to be instantly irritating.

'You see, Mr Archer. You will fall at the first fence. The judge will want to know how you intend to financially support the children if you are going to stay at home to look after them.'

'Will the judge ask the mother the same question?'

Mr Horsham continued in his matter of fact way. 'It will be presumed that the mother already had the majority of the parenting responsibilities from the beginning so it is more prudent and of course in the best interests of the children that it should remain that way.'

He was impressively rehearsed. It was the first time I heard the phrase, *in the best interests of the children* and would come to loathe it.

'Best interests of the children, my ass, best interests of the mother.'

Mr Horsham squeezed out from behind his desk and walked over to a water dispenser in the corner of the room. I looked around his office at the photos on the wall. There were a few pictures of him in younger, thinner days posing in a graduating gown or with goggles on his forehead on the skiing slopes. Also positioned between the photographs were different framed accreditations, which hung like gold discs in a recording studio. I felt quite sure that my life and Mr Horsham's had taken entirely different paths. No doubt he had been to a posh school that had the reputation for rowing and physics, while kids at my school were known for starting fires and end of term punch-ups. I asked him a question as he offered me some water in a plastic cup. 'Do you have any children?'

'Hell, no', he laughed. The short interlude seemed to have weakened the tense atmosphere. He squeezed back into his seat again, this time with a friendlier smile.

'You will get visitation rights,' he stated with optimism. 'Which means the law now protects your right see your children.'

'I'm allowed to see my own children?' I blurted in fake surprise. 'What's the point if they are in Germany.' Mr Horsham looked perplexed.

'Are your children in Germany?' I nodded and unburdened myself of my situation up to date. To his credit he listened patiently and only once looked at the ever-moving hand of the clock. Then when I had become repetitive in my ranting he gestured for me to stop.

'Mr Archer, I think it is only fair to mention that you have exceeded your free 30 minutes consultation.' He leaned forward. 'If you want me to represent you in your divorce and secure visitation rights over your children, I'll be happy to oblige. But if your children are in Germany, legally speaking my hands are tied.'

I quickly interrupted. 'I know, I know, but if the children were back in England, if I could get them back home. Could you help me get custody?'

'We don't call it that anymore.'

'Ok, parental control.'

'It's more likely to be visitation rights.'

'But could you try?'

'Not if they are in Germany,' he insisted. 'You will have to go over there. Although the Germans are a pretty liberal bunch and you'll probably be granted visitation rights over there too.' I was angered by the sudden offhand comment.

'So I have the right to visit them but not the right to determine where they live?'

Mr Horsham knew better than to continue. So he smiled and looked purposely at the clock before saying, 'If you wish to book an appointment or indeed you wish to continue now I will be obliged to charge you an hourly fee. If not Mr Archer, may I wish you the best of British luck.'

'How much?'

I WALKED BACK THROUGH THE waiting room that was now full with a new set of worried faces. I did not have the finances to ask Mr Horsham any more questions and I could see no walls in his office that needed plastering. So I walked outside with the words 'visitation rights' and 'in the best interests of the children' rattling in my skull.

A man who I had not noticed in the waiting room followed me out. He tapped me on the shoulder and reached out a bony hand to shake mine. He looked skinny and unwell with dark rings around his eyes yet could not have been any more than thirty.

'You may not remember me,' he said, 'I've aged a bit, not surprisingly with what I've been going through.' I did not take the bait and instead apologized for not recognizing him. He graciously waved it off.

'I saw you in the solicitor's office,' he said, 'I was sitting in the back.' He then took a card out of his pocket handed it to me.

'If you are here for what I think you are here for, then you may need support, we have to help each other,' he said politely.

'Support?' I questioned the word. He allowed me to read what was on the card. Our eyes met briefly then he was gone.

'All good men have to do for evil to exist is nothing.'

Chapter 6

As soon as I stepped in my house I noticed a large brown envelope on the mat. It was different to the other junk mail that had accumulated. It felt crisp and stiff to the touch. I needed a knife from the kitchen to slice it open.

At the top right hand corner of the single watermarked page was the government crest of The House of Commons. The Right Honourable Simon Steed, no doubts still basking in the stare from Mrs Thatcher's portrait, had been as good as his word. There were only two paragraphs, the first of which was straight to the point: *Your children may have been taken out of the country illegally and therefore in breach of the 'Hague Convention' act....*

At the bottom of the page was a telephone number followed by instructions: *please call, most urgent.* I lunged for the phone. Within two rings the call was answered.

'Mary Higgins.' Her voice was young and I imagined a teenager. She immediately recognised my name, which I found impressive then foreboding. She asked me to start from the beginning, which I did, although she soon cut in when I began to tell her how Eva and I had met.

'From the beginning of the abduction?' she insisted. It was a serious word, *abduction,* and my voice wobbled. I explained as best I could and soon realised that there wasn't much to say. Eva had taken the children on holiday and hadn't come back.

'Did you agree to this?'

'The holiday yes, them staying in Germany, never.' There was a long pause. I felt compelled to speak.

'I just want my children back.' I knew I sounded pathetic yet I hoped this may help reinforce her resolve.

'My office is here strictly to help implement The Hague Convention in cases where children may have been illegally taken from their country of origin. It applies to every country that has signed up to The Hague convention, which includes Germany. Its ruling,' she continued in a rehearsed fashion, 'its ruling supersedes all court procedures. You may have a legitimate case in your situation Mr Archer and you may,' she stressed the word *may*, 'be able to force the return of your children to England. But,' she paused again for breath, 'But, that doesn't mean you can keep your children here once they have returned. It will then be in the hands of the English courts to decide what is in the best...' I finished the last few words with her, 'interests of the children.' She was momentary put off by our joint recital.

'Mr Steed has informed me,' she continued, 'that your wife intends to divorce you in Germany?' I noted that she used the word 'me': My God, I thought, is it just her in that department? I had imagined a large office full of desperately serious people sitting at rows of desks. I felt suddenly vulnerable again.

'Yes,' I said, 'but I don't know exactly when. I haven't translated the whole letter that was sent to me. It's in German.'

As I spoke I was using my foot to sift through the junk mail on the doormat while keeping the phone firmly pressed to my ear. There under a local newspaper was another unusual envelope, this one with an express delivery sticker. I opened it while continuing to listen to her instructions and felt embarrassed at my lack of preparation. As I scanned over the translated letter she recited the numbers of two lawyers who lived in-and-around Ahrensburg and spoke English: Herr Bauer and Herr Lehmann.

She seemed happy to chat and as I had suspected, she was working alone in a small office in Westminster, a twenty-three-year-old graduate with my children's futures in her hands.

'When you get to Germany, you must show your lawyer the letter I have sent you. There are instructions in German at the bottom of the page. It informs who ever is representing you to telephone our office in Berlin. I will have already warned our Berlin office of your impending call.'

I scanned the page of the M.P.'s letter and found the instructions. I was now kneeling on the floor with both letters laid out in front of me. Her voice became suddenly stern. 'Mr Archer, do not show anyone the letter until you and your wife are just about to go to court. If her lawyers get wind of The Hague Convention your wife may be advised not to turn up so as to avoid its ruling. Don't tell anyone about the letter until the last minute.'

'Can I tell my German lawyer?' It had only just dawned on me that I would need one.

'Definitely not your lawyer, well, not until you have your wife in court or at least around an official negotiating table.'

Then I quickly browsed the translated letter.

'My God,' I said, 'the court date is set for the day after tomorrow.'

Chapter 7

I SQUEEZED MY EYELIDS CLOSED at the exact moment the wheels of the aircraft bumped onto the runway at Lübeck international airport. A ripple of applause came from the back of the cabin and I wondered if it was the pilots first time or if, like me, the passengers were petrified of flying and just relieved to be alive.

The stark German landscape of fields of stubble and distant silver birch trees began to slow as it passed the cabin window. The man seated next to me put his shoes on and I realised it was the odour of his feet that I'd originally attributed to the smell of burning wires.

Some uniformed men drove towards the plane in what looked like a golf cart with three trailers in tow. Then a beam of light shot in the cabin as the thick door was heaved open to allow us back into the outside world.

Perhaps it was the uniformed men in creaseless brown shirts who greeted disembarking passengers with official expressions, or the black and white war film I had watched two days earlier about an escaping British P.O.W., because when I waited patiently at the passport control, I gave the customs officer a look of panic when he beckoned he forward from the red painted line and demanded 'Show me your papers.'

I tried to act casual as the officer examined first my photo and then me. He clapped my passport shut and handed it back with a formal '*Danke schon.*' I walked to the carousel and watched the cases and bags shuddering by like orphan children waiting to be picked.

I took comfort in the few English voices that I could hear around me as I pulled my bag from the conveyer belt. Then I headed out through the sliding doors to walk the gauntlet of happy expectant people who scanned my face before finding someone else to wave to. By the time I had joined the line for a taxi, there were only German speakers and I felt very much alone.

I was exhausted from yesterday's last minute travel preparations. Dave had driven at lightning speed to make the flight, mounting the pavement outside the terminal.

After my plane had roared off into the sky, there was an uncanny silence around the single runway terminal that one would not normally associate with airports; birds could be heard singing in the fading light and beyond the car park from where I waited for a taxi, the tapping footsteps of a man walking his dog.

A large yellow Mercedes taxi replaced the one that had just sped away. I dragged my suitcase to the back of the car. As I went to reach for the handle, the boot automatically clicked open. I heaved my case in and walked to the car door. The driver, a huge man in a chequered shirt, whose stomach almost touched the steering wheel, was at first startled, then quickly realized with a smile my mistake and pointed me to the right hand side of the car. The taxi was spotlessly clean and smelt of polish. I slid into the seat.

'Wohin?' he asked.

'Ahrensburg Bitte.'

He tapped a thick finger on the taximeter. The red digital zeros shone out in the dull light. He stated a number, which I did not immediately understand and shrugged my shoulders.

'Do you speak English?' I asked. He pinched his forefinger and thumb together then said, '50 marks Okay?' I reluctantly agreed while desperately trying to work out the exchange rate. As he turned into the first road he spoke again.

'You are English?' he said. I nodded although I don't believe it was a question.

'You make holidays?'

'Sort of, well, not really,' I replied. The taxi driver grimaced in an effort to comprehend and I realized he too had a limited vocabulary.

'Yes, a holiday,' I stated clearly.

We headed through a built-up area. The reflections of the tall sleek German buildings reeled up the windscreen like a rewinding camera film. The most noticeable difference to English houses was the steepness of the roof pitch, which I would later learn was to prevent the accumulation of snow. The windows were larger too with no net curtains. People ate their dinner or watched television without a hint of inhibition to the viewing world outside. The taxi slowed to a stop in traffic. No more than three metres from where I sat was a large front window of a house. I could see a family seated around a table with the father cutting bread. He held the loaf upright and cut vertically towards him unlike in England with the loaf flat on the table cutting downwards. He handed large slabs to his children. I felt embarrassed and looked away, then sneakily look back again. I quite literally had a window on another family's life that in England would have been obscured from view. Germany is indeed another world, I thought, where these people live freely under the gaze of others.

The large taxi driver shifted uncomfortably in his seat and as we began to pull free from the traffic, he nudged me with his elbow.

'How long make you holidays?' he asked.

'Three days.'

'You English,' he snorted, 'you are crazy.' He whirled a finger to the side of his head. 'You are crazy,' he repeated.

I returned a questioning gaze, 'Why crazy?'

'In Germany six weeks is normal,' he announced, theatrically shrugging his shoulders. I was impressed.

'Two weeks holiday in England is normal.' The taxi driver snorted then chuckled. He was obviously enjoying the banter.

'In Germany I work and my wife work everyday, include Weihnachten but then six-week holiday, so okay.' I nodded my approval and his big forearm nudged me again.

'Two weeks is no holiday, that is why in England you are all crazy men on an island.' We shared a smile.

Within a few minutes we were out of the town and the yellow Mercedes glided onto the long uncongested autobahn that stretched out before us like a ribbon. I sunk back into my seat as the speed increased and we zipped passed larger vehicles as if they were standing still. Dave would like it here, I thought. It wasn't long before I first noticed the signs for Ahrensburg and my anxiety grew.

We glided off the autobahn onto a long smooth country lane bordered by neatly kept hedgerows. The evening was drawing in and the few isolated dwellings that we passed dazzled our eyes with their lights. Eventually we drove into the darkness of a tree-lined road and relied solely on our headlights. It gave me the feeling that the town of Ahrensburg was hidden within a forest. Then twinkling in the distance, illuminated by spotlights, I first noticed the pointed roofs that rose above the tree line like sharpened pencils. The Ahrensburg landmark of the Schloss slowly came into view. The taxi driver nudged me again, this time with an impressive nod saying 'German castle, you like?'

I raised my eyebrows theatrically as we turned off from the main road and rumbled over the cobbled street and drove directly past the fairy tale castle with its four witch hat turrets and surrounding moat.

A park that overlooked the castle held a memory. After a 22 hour flight from Australia, where I had met Eva backpacking, we had arranged to meet again in her hometown in Germany.

'We can meet by the castle with a moat,' Eva had said over the cracking phone line when I had telephoned from Sydney to say that I was leaving.

'Why, is there another castle without a moat?' I had joked. The bench was empty now as we drove directly passed it.

The evening darkness was almost complete so that the headlights showed the ripples of the newly painted white render as we came to a stop on the cobbles outside Hotel am Schloss.

It was a sleek modern building of dark red brickwork with uniform lines. The glass door of the entrance retained a shimmering reflection of the illuminated castle beyond. The electronically censored glass doors opened immediately as I stepped out of the taxi and onto the outside mat. The driver remained squeezed into his seat and flicked a switch and the boot popped open. After I had collected my bags I leaned across the seat and paid him 53 Deutsche Mark on the meter and felt guilty after his friendly banter that I could only leave a small tip.

He looked towards the hotel and gestured, rubbing his fingers and thumb together.

'*Sehr teuer*... much money,' he said. I shrugged my shoulders. He then handed over his business card before driving off, waving.

I dragged my bag across the hotel threshold and the glass doors automatically closed behind me leaving the sounds of the town outside.

A tall lady with a high-bridged nose stood behind a marble topped reception desk and spoke in clear precise English. 'Good evening sir, do you have a reservation?'

'How do you know I am English?' I asked.

She seemed to expect of the question. 'Because you got your own case out of the taxi.'

I approached the desk, leaving my bag by the door. As I got closer to the receptionist I noticed that she was considerably taller than I was.

I admitted to not having a reservation. She stood bolt upright as if balancing a book on her head and recited the room prices. She started with the lowest of 60 Deutsche Mark for a single room and continued upwards to 120 for a twin room. I quickly waved her into silence and asked with an embarrassed whisper. 'Do you have anything cheaper?'

'Sixty Deutsche Mark is our most inexpensive room but it does come with breakfast and use of the hotel sauna.'

'What if I don't use the sauna?'

'It's still 60 Deutsche Mark.'

'Or eat the breakfast?'

She spoke without emotion. 'There is a more competitive hotel on the other side of town.'

After a short silence she reached for a street map from under the counter and marked in red felt tipped pen a zigzag I should now to follow.

As I walked back to my suitcase I set off the door censors. The glass swiftly opened and the night air caused me to shiver. I turned to bid goodbye to the tall receptionist but her eyes were fixed on something below the counter.

I walked on the slippery cobbles to the traffic lights marked in felt tipped pen on my street map. My bag was heavy and pulled on my arm sockets. I resolved to pack more efficiently in future.

Across from the traffic was a tree-lined square situated in the middle of the town. Normally by day this would be filled with children running and playing while old people rested by the fountain and couples ate their lunch. Now, the square was empty except for the long dancing shadows cast from people in the brightly lit surrounding bars, no doubt drinking Weiss bier with large frothy heads. One person from inside the bar rubbed a hole in the steamed up window to look at me as I passed.

Further on I turned into a quieter road where the streetlights were darkened by the trees that grew alongside. There was an alleyway between a shoe shop and what I believe was a hardware store. A small sign was screwed to the wall, which announced in red letters, *Hotel Nr.6*. Underneath the sign was a hand pointing inwards. At the end of the passageway was a small bar. The outside tables were empty yet the bar inside was full of people. The light from the windows shone over the courtyard and the sound of banter and laughter increased as I approached the door. I recited my memorized words, *'Haben sie Zimmer bitte'* then pushed in.

Most of the people looked towards me as I struggled to hold the door open and pull my bag in. A man with a drooping moustache and shaggy long 70s style hair quickly approached and held the door. I thanked him in English before realizing, when he stepped over the bag that he was only trying to get out. I heaved my bag to the wall then found an empty bar stool.

A small shot glass was immediately placed in front of me and filled with a thick black liquorice-smelling drink. A short bald man with black round spectacles filled another and raised it to me. We tapped shot glasses and I swallowed with a grimace.

'Haben sie Zimmer?' I asked.

'I have many rooms,' he answered then added, 'Would you like one?'

'Yes please.' I was very much relieved to be speaking English. He looked towards my bag standing alone by the wall.

'Single room,' he stated.

'Yes please, your cheapest …. with no sauna.' Two men seated close by laughed. Yet the gentleman behind the bar did not join in and instead stretched his hand over the counter and shook mine warmly.

'My name is Herr Ovel. This is my hotel. You are welcome. For the cheapest it's 27 Deutsche Mark per room… We have no saunas.' I nodded my approval.

'But first,' he continued, 'before I show you to your room, one more I think.' He then proceeded to refill our glasses as well as the shot glasses of the two men next to me. We all held them in the air together before downing them in one. A glow warmed my cheeks and I felt accepted.

Across the small courtyard were steps leading to the large doorway, which opened into a stairwell of a narrow spiral stairs. Herr Ovel led the way up, switching on the timer light as he passed. He hopped briskly up the worn and chipped marble steps. I struggled behind him with my heavy bag, of which Herr Ovel seemed professionally oblivious. I balance my heavy load on my shoulder like a bag of cement.

My room was at the very top of the three-storey hotel. The timer light had clicked into darkness long before I could struggle past each level. Herr Ovel had already opened the door of an attic room by the time I had arrived sweating and panting behind him. He dropped the keys into my open palm stating sharply that breakfast was between 8.15 and 9. I clicked my heels together and said 'Jawohl.' Herr Ovel looked at me sternly so I quickly stuttered into silence.

'When does the bar close?' I asked politely.

'When everybody stops drinking,' he answered. He then disappeared down the spiral staircase, hitting the timer lights on as he went.

The room of 27 Deutsch Marks could have easy been calculated on the amount of times a visitor is likely to bang ones head on the sloping ceiling. I made the uncomfortable discovery of this when first standing up to stretch. It was only possible to stand up straight when the skylight window was open. I peered out over the slate roof and could hear the sound of laughter from the bar rising up with the smell of tobacco. It was already dark but could not have been so late in the evening. I yearned to see my children. It was surely their bedtime. I wanted to tell them Daddy is here and kiss them goodnight.

I scanned over the rooftops wondering which house was theirs. They lived so agonizingly close. I knew it would be impossible to see them now without a formal agreement and I didn't want to start an argument with Eva, which would look terrible for me in court tomorrow. Court tomorrow, the very thought made me shiver.

My head was spinning, not just from the long journey but also the liquorice shots that I had quickly downed. I lay on top of the bed. The cover sheet and blankets were so tightly folded that it pinged like an elastic band; yet it was surprisingly comfortable. I wanted to drift into sleep but as usual, of late, my mind was turning with thoughts of solicitors, park benches, and my children so close I could call to them.

In a moment of rashness I quickly stood up and immediately clutched my head in sharp pain. Rubbing my head, I grabbed my keys and stepped out of the room closing the door behind me, instantly wishing I had noted where the hallway light was situated. With hands patting along the wall I inched my way in darkness towards the stairs, finding with relief the switch. The light dazzled my eyes when clicked on.

I was soon out in the courtyard and walking away from the sound of the people in the bar. I was back in the dimly lit street.

It was an easy walk to the tobacconist shop. I first hurried towards the level crossing of the railway tracks, which ran through the middle of the town, splitting it in two. The crossing barriers were painted white with little flashing lights around a Halt sign. I leaned against them for a while and allowed the breeze to clear my head. There was no need to cross as the tobacconist was situated on my side of the tracks. I had to merely walk parallel for a few minutes until I found myself looking down another street of shops. The bar that was next to the tobacconist was the only building to have lights shining out on the street. Then a little beyond, slightly jutting out, the painted figure of a man smoking a pipe. I had stayed in that apartment many times while visiting with Eva. In the still of night, when laying in bed it was possible to hear the ding ding ding of the level crossing before the rush of a passing locomotive. Yet now, standing alone at the top of the street looking down I was very much aware of how outside that world I now was.

I walked on, listening to the sound of my own footsteps. I passed the bar unnoticed, which only had a few people inside. On the other side of the tobacconist was the butcher shop; its empty window displays full of spotless stainless steel trays clean ready for tomorrow's produce. There was a narrow alleyway in between, which allowed access to the small gardens behind. I cupped a hand against the glass of the tobacconist window and peered in. In the darkness I could see long neck smoking pipes on the wall and bundles of tied newspapers on the floor yet to be sprung open.

Suddenly, a light from an upstairs window came on and lit up the pavement. I quickly jumped into the darkness of the alleyway. I stood in silence flattened against the wall until thankfully, darkness again. Without thinking I dashed out into the middle of the street and looked up searching for the faces of my children. In a vain pathetic hope, I reasoned that they might have been looking out of the window for me. Yet the two rooms above the shop were in darkness and I remembered that the living quarters of the apartment were at the back. A small gate led to the garden behind the apartment. It was never locked and creaked when I opened it.

The back door, which led to the apartment stairs, was now right in front of me. I had the sudden impulse to knock but thought better of it. The door had a small window of thick frosted glass. I could just make out the dull light at the top of the stairs. It flickered as somebody passed.

I heard a voice coming from the apartment and the shock made me step back. I strained to listen with my unbelieving ears. It was not the voice of Eva or her parents, too deep. It was unfamiliar; a male voice. I became uneasy on my feet and leaned back on the gate, which unexpectedly crashed closed. I quickly turned and ran, taking the only direction available to me and headed into the darkness of the garden.

I tripped over something: a flowerpot, a children's play bucket, I couldn't be sure. I felt grass beneath my hands as I stumbled and fell. Both rooms at the back of the apartment switched on illuminating the garden like a flood-lit football pitch. I rapidly rose to my feet and in three long strides made it out of the arc of light. There was a small fence at the end of the garden, which I vaulted with ease then found myself in the unlit service road that connected the back of all the shops. There was a large over grown evergreen bush close to the corner of the garden fence and I quickly nestled myself within it. Panting to catch my breath I looked through a gap in the foliage and spied up to the apartment windows. There were no net curtains to obscure my view although the height of the windows gave only a limited vision of the rooms above. I swore and cursed to myself. Had I heard correctly? Could the male voice possible been in my warped imagination?

An insect crawled down the back of my neck and I resisted the impulse to flatten it. I saw the top of a small blonde head run cross the room. I cover my mouth with my hand to stop myself from calling out my son's name. My eyes watered and I gripped hold of a branch as if squeezing my mother's hand in the dentist.

Then I felt something gently touching my ankle and the sound of sniffing. I swiftly moved my leg and a dog began to growl. I sprang out of the bush to find a man in a large overcoat holding the leash of a barking dog.

'Du dreckiger Perverser,' he shouted. I immediately took flight as if triggered by a starting pistol. I sprinted out of the service road and hared towards the railway tracks.

I was soon walking back down the dark alleyway towards the small courtyard in front of the hotel bar. My hair had little bits of evergreen poking out and beads of sweat ran down my temples. I brushed myself down and slowed my breathing before pushing open the door.

My original bar stool remained empty so I took my place again. The two men I had shared the schnapps with were still seated at the bar. They stared curiously at my flushed face. One of them spoke in a strong German accent.

'You have a sauna, Ja?'

I looked at the Hoffmeister mirror behind the bar. My face was flushed red. I could now see what the two men were smirking at. I smiled back and they offered me a drink. We emptied our glasses then I bought them both one back. Herr Ovel had joined in with more complementary liquorice shots. We laughed a lot and patted each other on the back. We spoke a little about football with our limited vocabulary and mentioned players' names familiar to us all; I headed an imaginary ball into the goal behind the bar. I was drinking to forget. Had I really heard a man's voice?

Herr Ovel must have forgotten his promise on closing time and began to switch the lights off around me. I was soon the only one left; so bid Herr Oval auf Wiedersehen and staggered across the courtyard. I used the wall of the spiral staircase to slid up the stairs. Eventually I fell onto my bed having first smashed my head on the ceiling.

Chapter 8

THE SOUTHEND SEASIDE AMUSEMENT PARK by the southern English coast had reached the very last day of the season yet had begun to close up a week before. Most of the stalls were already boarded up with only a few desperate employees determined to rake in the last pounds and pence by selling the remaining toffee apples or ten shots on a crooked air rifle.

A cold autumn wind whisked through the park picking up the discarded litter and swirling it in circles. Only one major attraction, the log Flume, was still in operation although sadly the fiberglass log canoes bumped around the water trail and were hoisted up to the highest point of the ride without a single person in them to scream and yell as they cascaded down.

Both my children were enthralled by it and begged and tugged for me to let us all to go on. I looked at my watch; it was hours before I had agreed with Eva to take them back home.

A young attendant was at first reluctant to allow four and five-year-old children on the ride but with no other punters in sight, he agreed to let us all climb aboard. The children were thrilled at first but apprehension soon crept in as the metal bar pressed against their stomachs and they looked to me for reassurance. The hoist slowly clicked us to the top as we sunk back into our seat. Then a moment of calm as our fiberglass log drifted towards the edge with nothing but the sound of the wind and the cold fresh air to distract us. Then my children were gone. I searched around the log fume and looked over the side into the water, splashing and screaming their names as I drifted towards the edge. I panicked. I could see the water dropping off. Then they were back in their seats looking anxiously at me. I stretched from my seat and reached for them, and shouted 'I loved you!' Then all I could do was hold onto them and hope to hell that they would not let go of me. The front of the canoe began to tip.

I sat up with a start, the morning light glaring through the un-shaded skylight. I focused on the newly made dent in the ceiling and remembered last night's drunken entry. The side of my face throbbed where I had slipped off the bed during the night and lay with my face pressed against a radiator. I took stock of my surroundings; a tiny attic room with a framed photo print of the local castle hanging on the wall. A cloud passed the skylight giving momentary respite from the glare. There was a small radio clock on the bedside cabinet gently humming.

I remembered Herr Ovel's strict breakfast time slot. I had but twenty minutes remaining. I quickly located the third floor shower and was fortunate to find a discarded quarter bottle of shampoo. Five minutes later I was pulling my folded suit and shirt from my case and wishing I had not drank the night before. I was soon following the smell of coffee in my search for the breakfast room. I passed a large mirror in the hallway on the ground floor and caught an image of myself: I looked odd wearing a suit that was normally reserved for weddings and funerals. I wondered how people could bear to wear them daily. The smooth fabric felt shiny against my legs and the jacket restricting. Also, it was awfully creased from where it had been squeezed into my bag.

I walked towards the gentle sound of clinking cutlery. The dining room consisting of nine tables in three neat rows; only one table was occupied, by an elderly couple who bid me Guten

Morgen as I entered. The walls were clad in dark mahogany, which I realised was a favourite for the German interior; it was everywhere: the floors, the tables, the bar at the back of the dining area, even the shelf that ran high along the ceiling line, on which ornamental plates and cups were placed on dark, almost black stained timber. The dining room windows were customarily large, about a metre and a half high by three metres across in a single pane, which, because of its thickened glass, gave a slightly magnified view of the world outside. The floor level of the hotel dining room was somewhat higher than the pavement outside. I felt like I was in a theatre stall, viewing the actors who walked across the stage.

A little girl ran along the cobbles close to the window followed by her mother pushing another child in a pushchair. The girl was aged about four, similar to my daughter and was dressed in a bright banana yellow coat.

There was only one table in the dining room which still had bread rolls in a basket, so I assumed everyone else had eaten. I was not just hungry but starving. Apart from the free peanuts in the bar last night that I had caught in my mouth like a circus seal, I not eaten anything since leaving England.

A small round-faced girl appeared and pulled out the chair for me. I felt cared for until I realised she was probably in a hurry to get me started. She bid me guten Morgen in an accent I did not take to be German. I thanked her in English and she smiled before shuffling out of the room only to promptly reappear holding my breakfast platter of cold meats and a bowl of yogurt. I missed my porridge. Thankfully the coffee, the smell of which had helped lead me to the dining room, woke me up.

I heard the distant chime of church bells and I remembered the time. My God, I thought, I'm going to be late for my meeting with the German lawyer.

I took a quick slurp from my cup and immediately recoiled with a burnt tongue.

'Sehr heiß,' the waitress said mimicking my pain with a grimace.

'I'm late,' I moaned and stood up, instantly feeling dizzy. As soon as I was away from the table she began to clear up. Yet before I had made it to the spiral staircase the waitress was behind me, tapping on my shoulder.

'For later,' she said, offering a bread roll wrapped loosely in a napkin.

I was touched by another simple act of kindness. Like the friendly nudge from the taxi driver or the free shots in the bar, it helped to reinforce that if the German system was against me, the people certainly were not.

I arrived some minutes later at the offices of Otto Lehmann for our first face-to-face meeting. I ran all the way, skipping across the busy roads and along cycle paths where cyclists rang their bells in protest. Eventually I made it to the door of his offices.

I didn't expect Herr Lehmann to be bald; it wasn't what I had imagined when crying to him on the phone from England. This was the man who had said he could save everything so I assumed he would have a raging head of hair, like a lion.

After our initial meeting, when I'd noticed Eva's yellow dress from his office window and he told me about the Sioux Indians, Otto had informed Herr Bauer and Eva that there would be no negotiating before court. He instructed me to meet him outside the court, which was only five minutes away, while he quickly researched The Hague Convention.

I then spent some hours walking around the castle moat, sharing some of my bread roll with the ducks until the church bells chimed.

I found Otto pacing up and down on the small paved square, which lay outside of the modern red brick courthouse. Draped over his shoulders and flaying slightly in the breeze was a black gown: the official recognition of a German lawyer, which was required to be worn inside the courtroom. He was nervously running a hand over his bald head. Upon seeing me he cried out so loudly that some people that were pushing through the revolving doors of the courtroom turned to look.

'So, my English friend, you have made it. I was much afraid you were going to be late again.'

'I'm not late,' I explained shaking his hand firmly. 'In fact I am on time.'

Otto wagged a friendly finger. 'In Germany, for such important matters, we arrive early to make sure we will not be late. So in this way, you *are* late, but for England, yes, you have made it on time.'

I theatrically rolled my eyes and wanted to continue with a joke but Otto was quick to strike a serious tone and a solemn expression.

'Have you brought the letter?'

I went to take it out of my inside jacket pocket but he held onto my hand.

'I need to talk to you about that,' he said then paused for a moment before asking. 'I take it that you can understand a little German?' I answered in my best German sentence. *Ich spreche ein bisschen Deutsch.'* Otto nodded his approval and I felt somewhat impressive although in truth I only knew a few memorised sentences. It was difficult to admit to my lack of German when so many around me could speak English. A black dot appeared on Otto's lawyers gown, followed by another. He looked up to the sky.

'We better go inside, it's beginning to dribble.'

'Drizzle,' I corrected.

I followed Otto through the revolving doors of the courthouse then clicked across the tiled floor to the elevator. We entered together and stood silent while he checked his appearance in the mirror, tugging at his clothes, straightening his tie. Then, with a gentle ping and the flash of a floor number, the doors slid open.

I again followed Otto as he stepped out onto an ivory marbled floor area. A large arched window stretched its imprint over the little groups of people; each gathered around one particular person who held the conversation while they listened intently. To one side of the window, perched high on a column, the bust of Socrates cast its cold eye over everyone.

'We are in court number two,' Otto said, and then quickly beckoned me over to a small slit window, which although open would not allow a person's head to poke out. He began to look nervous and searched for a way to begin speaking.

'Have you seen your children since you've been in Germany?' he asked.

'No, not yet.' My cheeks flushed as I remembered seeing the top of my son's head the night before when hiding in a bush.

'That is good,' Otto continued, 'The judge will feel sorry for you.'

'Why does the judge need to feel sorry for me?'

Otto remained silent and ran a hand over his head. I burst into speech. 'What is it? Everything is going to be okay, isn't it? We have the letter. I can take my children home.'

'Yes, the letter,' he said. 'It is a sword with more than one edge, I had warned you of this when I spoke of the Indians.'

'Please not the Indians.' I was beginning to sound desperate I pulled out the envelope from my inside pocket and held it in view.

'This cites The Hague Convention and she is in breach of The Hague Convention. The law is on my side. This comes straight from Berlin. My Member of Parliament Simon Steed helped me sort it out and he knows Margaret Thatcher.'

My voice had become louder and other people who were in similar huddles were beginning to look up. Otto hushed me down with his hands and answered in a half whisper.

'Yes, yes you are right, for sure.' He waited until I had calmed. 'But also you are wrong,' he continued. 'The law, I believe in both our great countries can be like this.' His courtroom stare told me he had more to say.

'The Hague Convention states that if you take a child from its country of origin without the permission of both parents then that child or in your case, children, must be returned to their country of origin before any custody can be argued.' He looked at me and raised his eyebrows.

'I know this because I have been reading my law books for the past hour in my office and on the telephone to Berlin, they have been most helpful.'

'I never gave my permission for my children to stay in Germany.' I sounded like a defensive child. Otto slowly shook his head.

'That is not exactly true,' he said. 'You did allow your children to come to Germany.'

'For a holiday,' I protested.

'But you did agree.'

I spoke through gritted teeth. 'For a holiday, not for life!' Again a few people who were standing nearby turned and looked towards us.

Otto spoke as if he was addressing a jury. 'So *perhaps*,' he stressed, '*Perhaps* you can understand that it may,' he searched for a word, '*appear* that your children were not taken out of England unlawfully.'

I was taken aback and steadied myself against the small windowsill. I looked out of the tall castle slit window over the town of Ahrensburg. It had indeed begun to rain and the cobbled streets were washed clean by the downpour and empty of people. I answered while still looking out of the window.

'I'm not leaving this country without my children.' Otto remained silent and stared intently at me.

'I've bought plane tickets for the children,' I continued, 'and they have play school on Monday. I've cleaned their bedrooms.'

Otto put a hand on my shoulder, which made me gulp. He spoke in a soft yet still authoritative tone. 'If we go into that courtroom I do not believe I can prove that your children were taken unlawfully out of England. And even if I could, what then, your wife and children will return to England only to divorce you. She will be granted custody because mothers are always granted custody, and have the right to leave England with the children. Then they will be back in Germany only this time you will have no formal agreement for you to see your children.'

Otto allowed the information to sink in. My head was spinning.

'But I have the letter. They are my children.'

'They are her children too.'

'They are English.'

'Half English.' My voice began to croak. Otto waited expectantly. He looked serious to the point of mournful.

'So what are you telling me Otto?'

'I can tell you nothing,' answered Otto quickly. 'I can only advise.' Again he placed a hand upon my shoulder. 'Be brave, my English friend, and let your children stay in Germany.' It took a second for me to process. I recoiled from his touch.

'This is all wrong. This is complete bollocks!' I shouted. 'What about The Hague Convention, father's rights, equality? It's all a load of bollocks.' My voice echoed around the forum. Everybody stopped and stared.

For the first time I realized why the windows were so small; it was to prevent people from jumping out. A security guard appeared at the top of the stairs next to the lifts. I stormed through the crowd and headed towards the shiny silver elevator doors, which remained closed. The guard happily pointed towards the stairs and I ran.

I pushed through the revolving doors and out into the cobbled courtyard. The rain came down heavily in my face and I blinked as I search for a direction in which to run. I hurried along one side of the road under the shelter of the shopkeepers' red and blue-striped canvas canopies.

Eventually I slowed and stopped outside a small coffee shop. With no home to run to and a hotel whose cleaners would surely be everywhere, I quite literally had nowhere to go. I found myself staring at a window display of elaborately decorated cakes. The cafeteria looked warm inside. I pushed open the glass door. The seating area was mercifully empty of customers.

The rain had soaked through to my shirt so I removed my jacket and placed it on the back of a chair. A thin middle-aged waiter was soon by my side and made a remark about something that I presumed must have been the weather or at least that's what it would have been, if we were in England. He then held a pen to a small pad. I was in no mood to attempt to speak in German.

'I would like a cup of tea please.'

The waiter answered immediately in English. 'Would you like that with lemon?'

I answered harshly. 'Milk.'

The waiter raised an eyebrow although he did not look up from his notebook. '*Einen moment*' he replied flatly before walking off. I sat at the small round table and looked out of the window; the rain cascading down in lines from the overhead canvas. A familiar figure hurried past the window holding his lawyer's gown over his head; a few seconds later he returned and cupped a hand upon the glass. Within moments he was standing on the doormat inside the cafeteria, shaking off the rain. The thin waiter approached. They spoke in quick German before Otto was shown to the table. Surprisingly he took a table close to mine instead of joining me. Our eyes met and he smiled again yet neither of us spoke. Some moments later the waiter walked up to me carrying a cup of tea that he settled carefully on my table. Otto waited for the waiter to disappear behind the counter before turning to talk to me.

'Can I ask you just this one question? I am very curious.'

I stirred my tea before replying tonelessly. 'If you must.'

Otto sighed with relief and took my answer as an invitation to join me, quickly pulled up a chair at my table.

'I am very curious,' he repeated. The waiter returned and after a moment of confusion, placed a cup of steaming coffee in front of Otto at our table. There was silence between us again while we both concentrated on stirring our drinks. Otto is a solicitor; I thought, he knows how to wait.

'Ok, I give up,' I said. 'What makes you so curious?' Otto took a sip of his coffee before beginning.

'What is this *bollocks* you speak of?' he asked. 'My English is not so good. I grew up in the east on the other side of the wall. Russian is my second language. But I am a fast learner and listen to English radio all the time. Yet I have never heard this word before. You said, "it was all bollocks". What is *bollocks*?'

I laughed out loud and Otto at first seemed relieved then looked at me quizzically, and I wondered whether he thought I was mocking him.

'It's not a real word really,' I said. 'It's just slang. It means "what a load of rubbish". When you say *it's a load of bollocks*, you mean *it's a load of rubbish*.' Otto began to nod his head knowingly.

'Ah I see. This is very interesting. So when something is rubbish, it's the bollocks.'

'No,' I corrected. 'If you say "it's the bollocks", that means it's really good, but if "it's a <u>load</u> of bollocks" then it's really bad.' Otto ran a hand over his head,

'I don't think I completely understand but I will learn this. Every day a new thing you learn.'

I sat back in my seat and sipped my tea. I was beginning to like Otto; he was creeping up on me. His sincerity and honest unabashed way was infectious. I had, up until now, looked upon him as a tool for hire; a necessary service. Liking him had not, indeed did not need, to come into it. Yet as I watched him stir his coffee, muttering the different expressions to himself, committing them to memory, he was, without a doubt, growing on me.

Outside the rain had almost stopped and the few people that passed had their umbrellas down. Otto made ready to leave.

'We must go back,' he said. 'I was able to move your court time but only by a few hours. We must attend. It would look terrible for you as a father if you did not.'

I forced a smile, then spoke softly while looking down at my empty tea cup. 'This is like a nightmare,' I muttered. 'I don't know how I'm going to leave them behind. I really love my children, you know. I love them so much it hurts.' Otto stooped his head down further than mine so as to make direct eye contact and draw me up.

'Then we must go in the courtroom and tell them so. I know this judge. As I have told you before, I have a brick in her wall. Like me, she has also come from the other side of the Berlin wall.'

*

HERR MÜHLEMAYER WAS ONE OF the oldest judges on the Schleswigholstein circuit, often used as a relief judge to fill in on rescheduled court hearings. He was known for his harshness and had been encouraged many times by more progressive, moderate judges to take up his retirement and enjoy his holiday home in

Bavaria. Yet Jürgen Mühlemayer insisted on continuing to serve the courts if only to fulfil his promise to his dying mother and protect other mothers, who like his own, had been abandoned and left penniless when he was at the tender age of nine.

He was most noticeable amongst other, much younger judges, in that he was seldom seen unaccompanied, always insisting on having two *female only* courts staff to help him shuffle slowly to his seat at the head of the court.

Otto relayed this story to me in nervous whispers as we stood in reverent silence in court number two.

'This is not good,' Otto whispered. 'We have been given the worst judge.'

'I thought you said you had a brick in his wall.'

'Her wall,' Otto insisted. 'Because I changed the court time we have been given a different judge. This morning we could have had Justice Heinrich, who is very sympathetic towards me.'

I watched Justice Jürgen Mühlemayer puff and breath with exaggerate labour while being helped into the elevated seated position behind the dark oak table. He thanked the two female staff, awkwardly holding onto one of the women's hands preventing her from leaving too quickly. His hair was almost white and he wore thin black glasses, which magnified his eyes. His eyebrows were wildly bushy and unkempt. Also he had an annoying habit of clicking his mouth after he swallowed.

Momentarily he looked up at Otto who gave a respectful, anxious nod in return to which the judge did not reciprocate.

The courtroom was modern and windowless with bright fluorescent lights, which bounced off the stark white walls. Apart from the eagled crest that hung above the judge, there was nothing on the walls. Our table, behind which we were now permitted to be seated, did not face the front but was aligned parallel to the opposing legal team. In such cases the tables are purposely placed in this way to encourage debate between the two sides, Otto explained. Yet for now the table opposite remained most conspicuously empty.

There was a loud clang and the large door of the courtroom was pushed open. A court official scurried across the room. She was a thin woman in her sixties and dressed completely in black apart from the silver chain that hung around her neck to match a silver bridge on her thin triangular spectacles. She whispered loudly in the judge's ear. I asked Otto what was happening but he quickly silenced me with his hand while he strained to listen.

While the court official spoke, the judge looked first at Otto then scornfully at me. His stare burnt holes into my head. Otto quickly took some papers out of a suitcase and tapped them together. Panic had begun to creep over me. My heartbeat increased. I was in a slow car crash.

'Let's delay the court hearing again,' I said hopefully. 'Then we can get the good judge.'

Otto looked irritated. 'And for what reason do we give?' I looked over to the empty table opposite.

'She hasn't turned up?'

For the first time Otto spoke with genuine agitation. His brow was knitted and the muscles around his mouth tightened.

'I have already overheard the court official tell the judge that your wife will be late because she had to rearrange childcare after being sent away from the first hearing when you walked out. This is Germany, everybody follows the rules, we seldom re-arrange, we are never late. This does not look good for us.' I buried my face in my hands realizing the stupidity of running out.

Then the doors behind us opened and the whole court stopped and watched the procession walk in. I had not seen Eva since the day at the airport, the day they went to Germany. Louise had been perched on Eva's hip and Sebastian, who had insisted on standing, held Eva's hand as they walked. I watched and waved from behind the barrier while their bags were fed through the scanner, and one by one they walked through the metal detector. I'd stood ready to wave whenever my children looked back, which was often, their eyes still searching for reassurance. Eventually they were lost in the mass of bodies in the busy, bustling world beyond security. The last face I'd seen was Eva's; unlike the children, she had not looked back until the very end. She'd given a forlorn half smile, that, only weeks later after the phone call telling me that she was not to return, did I fully comprehend.

WALKING IN FRONT WAS THE newly appointed Frau Meier and not Otto's friendly adversary, Herr Bauer. Both Otto and myself were taken by surprise. Frau Meier, as we would soon learn, was a hotshot lawyer from Hamburg. She was in her fifties and only represented female clients. She had a work motto printed on expensive business cards, which read 'Gleichheit für frauen, *Equality for women*'. Under her lawyer's gown she wore a suit with trousers and flat brogues. Her hair was styled in thick auburn curls that seemed so fixed with hairspray that it did not bounce as she walked; it could have been a wig.

Frau Meier made no attempt to avert her gaze and scanned over both Otto and myself. I felt very uncomfortable, like the bully had just entered the classroom.

Eva followed closely behind, rhythmically in step. She was dressed in complete contrast to Frau Meier and wore that yellow dress with her long blonde hair hanging straight and silky past her shoulders. She looked healthy and good; her high cheekbones shiny. Her piecing blue-grey Germanic eyes never rose high enough for anyone to make contact except for a glancing, shy smile that she afforded the judge. She looked angelic with her soft stepping gait, like a queen in procession. It was impossible to look away. I could not see Otto's mouth from where I was standing although I am sure, like mine, it was open.

I HAD, SINCE THE PHONE call, scorned any loving thoughts towards Eva. It seemed impossible to feel love towards the very same person who was causing the pain. She had taken my children, split my family; she was the root of my agony, the reason for me being in Germany and my children being there too. I hated her. Yet there, in the courtroom as I watched her tuck her hair behind her ear, I knew at once that she was nervous too. I wanted to hug her and tell her to be strong, tell her I was proud of her. My heart was pounding and my eyes unable to look away. I spoke my thoughts, not conscious that they were aloud and completely audible to all those in the courtroom. 'My God, I still love her.'

Otto quickly grabbed my arm. 'It is not permitted in the court for you so speak directly to the opposition.' Then he whispered, 'I understand.'

Both on the opposing table smiled to themselves, although Frau Meier's grin never reached her eyes as she wallowed in *schadenfreude*.

I looked over to Eva; our eyes had yet to meet. She continued to look down like a shy frightened girl although in reality, I knew Eva would be dying to look up at me too. Someone, I suspected the frosty lady seated next to her, had coached her, and I, fool that I was, had gifted her this judge.

Everyone waited in silence while Judge Mühlemayer continued to read through the papers, his thick glasses showing his eyes moving steadily across the lines. The court official, who had entered to talk to the judge, now took a seat next to him in a chair substantially lower in height. There was more silence.

Eventually the court official was prompted by a nod from the judge. She in turn looked over the silver brim of her spectacles at

Otto who stood up and cleared his throat. He spoke without looking down at his papers; first addressing the judge and then the opposite table. His hand gestures were wide and extravagant and come the end of his short speech he looked at me while mentioning my name, which, to my alarm, was the only part of the speech I had truly understood. He then sat down and Frau Meier stood up and did the same but with less panache, often looking at the table as she spoke. I took hold of Otto's arm and frantically whispered.

'I don't understand a bloody word.' Otto's eyes widened.

'What do you mean you don't understand?'

'I don't understand any of it.'

Otto looked incredulous. 'But you said you speak a little German.'

I shrugged my shoulders like an embarrassed child. 'No, I can say the sentence, *I speak a little German in German* but that's about it…and order some food. I'm English, for god sake what did you expect.'

In all of our conversations Otto had always spoken English. We had never once tried to converse in German since our very first phone conversation.

Otto quickly stood up before Frau Meier had finished speaking and whatever he said it rendered her into silence. Then everybody looked to the judge for his reaction. He had a moment of contemplation then swallowed with a click of his mouth before speaking in a croaky frail voice. Everybody strained to hear. Halfway through their muted conversation the judge stared directly at me so that Otto felt the need to lean backwards so as not to impede his view. His magnified eyes were scolding. When the judge had finished speaking Otto put a hand on my shoulder and was about to make an address when the frosty lady, rose from her seat. She spoke loudly and so quickly that it was impossible to distinguish the gaps between the sentences. Her voice pitch increased and then suddenly at the end of her rant she swapped into English while looking at me.

'How you say in England, *You are playing for time.*'

I did not answer; the sudden sentence in English had taken me by surprise. Otto interrupted and addressed the court, mercifully also in English.

'If the court will allow, I would like a moment to speak with my client.' Frau Meier became indignant and spoke loudly, gesturing towards Eva who shook her head.

The judge raised his hand and all were immediately quiet.

'*Nur ein Minuten,*' he said.

Otto turned in his seat to face me and cupped his hand to shield his mouth. His whisper was intense. ' I am very...'Otto searched for the word '...Verlegen.., embarrassed. I should have asked for a translator and it would look very bad for us again if we stop the court to have one appointed.'

'I'm sorry,' I pleaded, 'I thought you knew.' Otto muttered to himself, shaking his head. Then, as if a switch had been flipped, he looked at me with a clear fresh smile.

'It is my mistake; I have been unprepared but it is not for the spilt milk to be crying. I will tell the judge that we do not intend to use The Hague Convention and argue for the return of the children to England, so perhaps we do not need a translator for this court hearing after all.'

'This court hearing,' I stuttered in disbelief. 'Do we need another court hearing?' Otto suddenly lurched forward so that the gap between us was even closer. 'This court hearing is to agree upon where your children live. The next will be about the divorce.' Otto spoke loud enough for Eva to hear. She looked up and for the first time out eyes met. I wanted to smile, even pull a funny face, anything to show her how easily I was taking it all when I

72

clearly was not. But the court was watching, in particular the lady seated next to the judge who stared intently at me. Frau Meier nudged Eva and drew her eyes away into a whispered conversation. Otto regained my attention.

'You must trust me. I will tell the judge that you are happy for the children to stay in Germany…'

'But I'm not happy.'

'I will tell the judge that you are okay with the children staying in…'

'But I'm not okay.'

'Then I will say,' he searched for the words 'you reluctantly agree…'

'I do not agree.'

Otto replied sharply. 'You mad men on an island! Do you not understand?' Otto's voice had broken from the whisper. 'You are *never* going to get your children back to England. Never. Not even for a holiday unless you agree to them staying here first. Understand this.'

I was stunned by his harshness and slumped into my seat. He put his hand on my shoulder and levered himself up to address the court. At first he began to speak in a calm voice, which slowly became harder. It was fascinating to watch when I didn't understand the words: the heightened inflexions, the waving hand gestures, the intenseness of the people watching. Yet inevitably I zoned out; I didn't understand. I allowed my gaze to stray across the room to Eva.

She, like all the others in the courtroom was fixed on Otto's oration. I felt or rather I hoped that she was concentrating hard not to look back at me.

Was this the same woman I had once washed down with a sponge? Squeezing warm water over her naked body to rinse her clean from the sweat and blood of labour. Our first baby, wrapped by the midwife in a warm towel was placed within her arms and we giggled like children. 'Look what we've made,' I said. I wished she had the courage to look over at me now.

Suddenly Otto was staring down at me and I quickly realised that his language had swapped from German to English.

'My client has already agreed,' he said 'that it is in the best interests of the children that they remain in Germany.'

I shot a glance from Otto to the judges and then to Eva.

'I do not agree,' I stated.

Otto's cheeks flushed and he was momentarily lost for words. The judge glared at Otto with his magnified eyes and the court official shook her head. It was Eva who broke the silence by slamming her hand on the table.

'Oh Richard!' she said loudly. Frau Meier quickly began to hush Eva.

Otto remained standing although he stooped down to speak. 'I thought we had spoken about this. If they are going to stay anyway, it will look better if you agree with it.'

'If they are going to stay anyway, then it doesn't matter if I agree or not.'

Otto ran a hand over his shiny head. I reached out and tugged gently on his black gown.

'Please try and make the judge understand. I'm not trying to stop it anymore, I know I'll lose, but that does not mean I agree with it,' I whispered.

The judge cleared his throat to draw Otto's attention but to my surprise Otto raise a flat palm to the judge and urged me to continue.

'I don't want my children thinking I wanted this to happen. The system is rubbish; it's all a load of rubbish. Make the judge understand.' I spoke loudly knowing I was quite audible to everyone in the court.

Otto then faced the judge and gave a respectful nod.

'Will you allow me to address the court in English?'

The judge answered 'I will.'

'My client has every respect for the court's authority and knows that his children may now reside here in Germany.' Eva gave a huge sigh.

'But he wants the court to know that he does not agree with it. And if my comprehension of the English language serves me correctly, including what my client has taught me today, I think I am right in saying my client thinks it's all a load of bollocks.'

Chapter 9

THE STREETS OF AHRENSBURG LOOKED very different to me that evening. I strolled around at dusk just as the streetlights began to flicker on: the cold autumn air pressed against my face and I turned my collar up.

I was searching for the familiarity and sense of belonging that perhaps my children might now have with this town. I crossed a small bridge, which led to the train station. I thought of the old stone bridge in my own town in Chelmsford. It was always a place where people used to meet or say goodbye. Would my children, if they were to grow up here, now use this bridge in Ahrensburg as their meeting place?

I continued to walk towards the station and stopped by a small shop that sold games and toys. The large display window was covered in fingerprints about waist high. I assumed young children had pressed their hands against the glass as they marvelled at the newly assembled He-Man Starship Eternia. I wondered how long it would be before my son's fingerprints would be on the window. How long it would be before this town gave my kids a sense of belonging; the very same town where I could now barely remember my way back to the hotel.

A group of small youngsters, who I thought not old enough to be on their own, passed noisily on the other side of the road. They were screaming and shouting excitedly at each other amid burst of sporadic laughter. I stood and stared, looking for the faces of my own children amongst them, not expecting to see them personally but someone similar to them, someone that they might grow into.

One of the boys, wearing an orange bobble-hat returned my stare. The others soon noticed his attention to me. They immediately became quiet and hastened their pace. The smallest amongst them, a little girl at the back of the crowd who was skipping to keep up, beamed a smile before bravely calling out 'Guten Abend!' The rest of the group quickly followed her example and bid me good evening as well.

I was rather taken by their politeness and added a wave of my hand as I returned their greetings. The little girl almost stumbled as she continued to look back, frantically waving as she hurried to keep up.

I swallowed deep. I missed my own boy and girl so much. Apart from the top of my son's head when I had been hiding in the bush, I had not seen them for ages. I would have given anything at that moment just to kiss them goodnight. At least, I thought, I had only to wait until tomorrow to see them again.

After the court hearing that afternoon, while all of the solicitors were packing away their papers and filling their briefcases, Otto had prompted me to speak aloud to Eva while the judge was still in hearing distance. Eva was standing and listening to the intense whispers from Frau Meier. The judge, who was in the process of being helped to his feet by two female staff, was making to leave. I broke the silence and called across the courtroom.

'When can I see the children?' I asked pitifully.

The judge, whose job it could possibly be to decide the visitation agreement in the next court hearing, noticeably turned his ear to hear. Frau Meier knew better than to intervene.

'Tomorrow afternoon,' Eva answered flatly.

'Why can't I see them for the whole day? I only have tomorrow.'

Otto kicked my foot under the table and frowned. 'Just say yes.'

Eva glared across the room at me, forgetting to maintain her shy angelic appearance.

'We have already made arrangements to go to Hamburg with a friend in the morning,' she said, then added, 'You can pick them up at the shop at lunch time.' I curled my feet in my shoes and agreed with a grimace.

Otto seemed happy with the arrangements. A few minutes later, after we had left the courtroom and descended down in the lift, he proclaimed the hearing to be a success. 'We fight to live another day,' he said, ignoring my frown.

'Enjoy your children tomorrow and we will talk again before you leave,' Otto added. We parted outside the revolving doors. Otto quickly turned away, causing his black gown to spiral out. He waved without looking back.

From that moment, I had walked the streets; not wanting to go back to the hotel, not knowing where I was going until the very moment that I found myself standing outside the games shop watching the fading images of the children disappear into the darkness. I felt cold and headed back to the hotel.

Chapter 10

AFTER SPENDING A NERVOUS MORNING kicking about the hotel dodging the cleaners, I found myself standing at the top of the street. I could see people going in and out of the tobacconist shop. My time to see Louise and Sebastian had finally come. Yet at the last moment I felt unable to take another step.

I had spent weeks of sleepless nights visualizing the time when we would all run into each other's arms, like the final triumphant scene of a Walt Disney film. Yet, I stayed at the top of the street, in full view of the townspeople who gave me quizzical sideways glances as they walked by. I was unwilling to go any further because despite all, I had the sudden fear of rejection.

I did not doubt my children's love for me but I was uncertain as to their ability to comprehend the situation in their tender minds. At age four and five they had yet to grasp the true concepts of time and memory, of yesterday or the day before that; a week ago belongs to another world.

Would they still remember me as their father? Had I already become a stranger, a foreigner? Or worse still, did they somehow blame me for not being there? Had I, in their childlike reasoning, abandoned them? They are so young, I thought and everything had so quickly changed, perhaps their affection for me too.

It would be many months later that I could benefit from the advice of an English painter and decorator who had befriended me in an Ahrensburg bar on a different trip to Germany. He had noticed my difficulty in understanding the barman's broken English and offered to help. Over a frothy Weiss he told me his theory of keeping in touch with loved ones back in England.

'You have to phone at least twice a week, more if possible,' he advised. He had a strong Yorkshire accent that I found profoundly comforting in a place surrounded by German speakers.

'I phone the wife and children twice a week,' he continued. 'Once is not enough. You have to be in their routine as well as their hearts.'

An old man with a bellowing pipe stared at me as he puffed past like a steam engine. I must have looked quite conspicuous, standing at the top of the street, looking down, going nowhere. German people always seemed to be heading somewhere. Also, some of the ladies from inside the bakery were beginning to stare at me through the gap between the loaves of bread and flour dusted rolls. I shifted uncomfortably.

Then in the distance I saw a vision that made my face flush. I swallowed hard. I could see the little figure of a girl standing outside the tobacconist shop. She was no higher than the waste paper bin she stood next to: little Louise, wearing chequered trousers and a pink jumper, her arms folded and searching the faces of every man who passed her by.

I instinctively moved forward and started to walk towards her, slowly at first, my eyes fixed upon my little girl as she stood waiting and watching. As I approached she turned and recognized me. She pointed her finger towards me and looked back into the shop. 'Mein Pappa' she shouted, 'Mein Pappa.' She ran towards me, her feet moving as fast as she could, pigeon chest sticking out, knees raising high, arms pumping, with no fear of trip or injury. I crouched down to her level on the pavement ready to receive her as if bracing for a rugby impact. She jumped up at the last second and I rolled back with her in my arms. She had not forgotten me! She had not forgotten me.

Sebastian had watched all of this from inside the shop doorway, hiding behind the doorframe. He, like most small boys, had waited, his eyes searching through his scraggly blonde fringe for reassurance. I would have to go and find him first and coax him from behind the door. Walking with Louise now in my hip I crouched down and scooped him up with my other arm. I noted that they had both become heavier.

They giggled at each other from across my chest, their arms hooked around my neck like monkeys. They smiled like it was Christmas and once outside the shop I whirled around like a spinning top while they screamed with delight. They had not forgotten me.

There were people in the shop. I had seen their feet when I'd reached down to pick Sebastian up. Yet I purposely did not raise my eyes, and ignored them. Instead, I spoke loudly and clearly so that all around me could hear. 'Daddy's come to get you.'

When I finally looked back inside the shop I saw Eva's mother, standing beside the cash register. She was dressed in her white trousers and t-shirt with a printed tobacco slogan and was putting out a cigarette in an ashtray on the counter. Eva's father was standing behind the cash register, dressed more formally with a shirt and tie poking out from the top of his turtleneck sweater; he smiled and said hello in English.

I didn't answer. Instead I squeezed my children closer together so that all three of our heads were touching as I stared back at them both. I felt like being harsh and saying something defiant, but I was too happy and wanted to be gone.

'Where are your coats?' I asked them. They both wriggled free, scurrying back into the shop and picking up their coats and two little backpacks that had been placed behind the door.

'We want to go to the *schwimmbad*,' said Sebastian. I noted immediately the German word.

I looked around for a pushchair. Louis, I reckoned, would not last more than fifteen minutes on foot.

'Where is the pushchair?' I asked Eva's mother, who had already lit another cigarette and was now standing in the shop doorway. The one thing we had in common was that neither of us could understand the other.

I mimicked the back and forth motion of a pushchair although it could have been a lawn mower. I repeated the word slowly: 'P-u-s-h-c-h-a-i-r.'

A familiar voice came from the open window above the shop. I looked up but could only see the reflection of the passing clouds in the glass.

'Why do you need the pushchair, Richard? You are only going to make it muddy.'

'Eva.' I looked up and squinted. 'Why don't you come down?' I tried to sound casual although my heart was thumping.

'I knew you would cause a scene,' she said before slamming the window shut. I quickly began to help the children on with their coats. My hands were trembling. I looked into their eyes for my own reassurance.

Eva soon appeared from inside the shop holding a small tattered fold-up pushchair. Her hair was tied tight behind her head and she was wearing a tracksuit outfit, so I assumed she was about to go to the gym. She walked straight past her mother and up to me. There was a brief moment where our eyes focused on each other. I saw the small creases in the corner of her eyes, and the line of her unpainted lips.

'Here, you can use this one,' she said placing the stroller at my feet. 'My mother bought it at a second-hand boot fair so it doesn't matter if you get it dirty.'

My cheeks flushed and I stood up straight to face her.

'I am not a child too. Where is the new one that I bought two months ago? I want to use that one.'

'It's upstairs,' she replied, 'and I'm not carrying it all the way down here. It's too heavy.'

'Well, I'll go and get it.'

Eva was quick to answer, 'You are not to go inside. You don't live with us any more.' I was taken aback and my voice quivered as I spoke.

'Do I now have to wait outside? My children are living here but I can't go in?' Eva looked resolute and practiced. She stared straight into me.

'You can take them to the park,' she said, then added with her eyebrows slightly raised, 'just like all of the other fathers.'

And there it was; it had happened. In a blink of an eye, in a sentence, I had entered that other world and my heavy defenceless heart sank upon hearing her words. I had become a shadow of a father. In future, I thought, I would have to bring my own pushchair.

I knelt down to Louise and began to fumble nervously with the zip of her coat. In a moment of either pity or control, I do not know which, Eva's mother walked over to help my trembling fingers with the coat. I brushed her hand a side.

'Buy another dog,' I said. This was a cruel reference to the fact that their family dog had died some months previously and I had the growing suspicion that my children had filled the mournful gap. Eva spoke rapidly in German to her mother. It did not sound complimentary.

I picked both my children up in my arms and tried to look unfazed.

'We can walk. It's not far. We don't need the pushchair anyway,' I said. I leaned forward holding both my children in my arms so that Eva could kiss them goodbye. I could smell her skin; we did not make eye contact. I then turned and walked away.

Eva called after me in a gentler tone. 'Back in three hours.'

Chapter 11

A SHINY ALUMINIUM VENDING CART in the corner of the market lit up like a light bulb whenever the clouds parted to allow a flash of the sun to shine upon it. The sizzling sausages emitted a smell that acted like a pied piper tune and it was in this way that we were drawn towards the open market square.

A huge man wearing a cooking apron the size of a tablecloth was serving sausages that were griddled before the salivating customers. A beer crate had been placed in front of the cooking platform so that children could stand on tip toes and watch from behind the safety glass as their chosen sausages were griddled.

My children ran to take their place on the beer crate as it became apparent to me that they'd done this before. We each chose a different variety, and with a large greasy smile, the vendor soon handed us our chosen sausages in a small cardboard sleeve that served to save our fingers from burning. I found a low wall for us to sit on. We blew and bit into our würste.

'Did you miss me?' I asked. They both nodded while continuing to eat. Louise quickly swallowed so she could speak.

'I waited outside the shop for you.'

'And me,' Sebastian added.

'I know you did,' I said warmly. I so wanted to hear more; how they had missed my goodnight kiss, how they continually asked their mother where I was. But they were young, so this was enough.

I looked at my children sitting on the low wall with their feet barely touching the ground. I pitied them for their innocence. Perhaps now would be a good time to explain.

'Do you have anything you want to talk to me about?' I asked casually. They both continued to chew on their sausages. Sebastian shrugged his shoulders.

'You can ask me anything,' I added.

Sebastian swallowed before speaking. 'Where do sausages come from?'

'Well, maybe not questions about anything. Pigs I think. But don't you want to ask a question about Mummy and Daddy?' Louise stopped eating.

'I don't want to eat a pig,' she said, 'I like pigs.' They both looked at me with blank expressions while kicking their heels against the wall.

'Questions about why Daddy is not living with you and Mummy?' I said, my frustration was apparent in my voice. Sebastian obliged.

'Why don't you live with us any more?' Finally, I thought and took a deep breath.

'Mummy and Daddy both love you very much but we don't seem to be getting along at the moment.'

'Why?' asked Sebastian.

'Because!!' This was becoming more difficult than I thought and I searched my head for an example they could understand.

'Imagine,' I began, 'Imagine Mummy and Daddy are like a cat and a dog. Sometimes cats and dogs like being around each other and sometimes they don't like being around each other.' Louise perked up.

'Who is the dog?' she asked. I couldn't call their mother a dog, I thought.

'I'm the dog and Mummy is a beautiful cat,' I said.

'But cats are scared of dogs,' offered Sebastian.

'It doesn't matter who is the dog or the cat, that's not the point. Mummy could be the dog.'

'Mummy's a dog?' asked Louise with a frown.

'No, Mummy isn't a dog,' I said. 'Don't tell Mummy I said she was a dog. Oh it doesn't matter anyway. Just finish your sausages.'

'I'm not eating a pig,' protested Louise.

'You're a pig,' laughed Sebastian.

'Dad, Seb called me a pig.' This was far more difficult than I had anticipated.

After cleaning their hands and face with a tissue I took them both by the hand and strolled around the market square, our faces warmed by the occasional appearance of the sun. I bought three apples from a market vendor who quickly spun them in a bag. I pushed them into one of the children's backpacks, which I now had to carry along with my own.

I felt terribly unprepared and regretted rushing out of England with nothing but the court case on my mind; yet in truth, I'd defiantly reasoned that to have prepared for anything other than the immediate return of the children to England was somehow giving in to the possibility of them staying.

In the future I would be more organized: baby wipes, spare underwear, fruit drinks, socks, colouring books, plasters and a blanket for the cold. I would learn my needs through my mistakes: cold hands, next time I would bring gloves. Step in a puddle, a dry spare pair of socks appeared from out of my backpack. After many trips I became an efficient daddy machine with a bag packed full of things for every eventuality; all of which would have to be carried on the plane from England.

I would also learn the lay-out of the town of Ahrensburg; not as a visiting tourist but as a father with no home to take my children. I would learn the routes through the parks and the forests, with the different bus shelters and bridges to stop under when it rained. I became familiar with the stores in the large shopping areas where we could linger inside without buying anything when it was cold. The pizza restaurant was a favourite, because when seated upstairs we could go an hour unnoticed before I had to purchase anything.

When the town was completely closed we strolled from shop window to shop window each choosing an item to furnish our imaginary house: right up to the very last minute until they had to be returned to the flat above the tobacconist:

It was a short walk from the market place to the swimming baths, which I found on the map that the tall receptionist had given me in the expensive hotel. Louise became reluctant to walk and soon rested heavy on my hip. I regretted my show of defiance and wished I had taken the pushchair.

Das Ahrensburg Schwimmbad was a clean, new building that consisted of a huge dome with a glass frontage. The smell of chlorine wafted out with every wet haired child and adult that pushed through the polished doors holding a damp towel under their arm.

I led my children in and was immediately taken by the heat of the reception area. Both were eager and excited. We joined a line of people at an entry kiosk and soon reached a stern lady seated behind the counter. I handed her the largest bank note and held up three fingers. She asked me a question in brisk German, which of course I did not understand. I instinctively spoke in English.

'Three for swimming please, two children, one adult.' Again she spoke in German then waited for an answer. So I pointed at the swimming pool that could be seen through the window behind her.

'We want to go swimming' I repeated but again she said what I presumed to be the same question. The people in the line behind me were becoming agitated and bore their eyes upon me until mercifully somebody spoke in English. I turned to see an elderly lady. She was impeccably dressed in a white skirt and blouse buttoned to the top. For an older person she stood with an extremely straight back and her silver hair was so tightly pinned behind her head that it pulled back the wrinkles on her face. She held the hand of a little boy who looked to be around the same age as Sebastian. He stood beside her in silence.

'She wants to know how long you wish to swim for. You must pay by the hour,' said the old lady in near perfect English.

'One hour.' I faced the receptionist with a single finger pointing towards the sky. I then turned and thank the helpful lady with an animated bow of my head that I hoped would shame the impatient people in the line. I received my change in a tray on the counter along with three blue plastic coins.

The children grabbed a coin and ran ahead through a turnstile. By the time I had caught up, they had settled their little backpacks in a small room with a wooden planked bench and overhead lockers, not unlike a football changing room. Sebastian was quick to kick his shoes off and undress but Louise, although being equally excited, struggled with her shoelaces; I duly took charge. I was relieved and grateful to find that both had been prepared and were already wearing their swimming outfits underneath their clothes. I contributed this good deed to Eva or possibly her mother and felt ashamed for my *buy another dog* comment.

Louise began to giggle while sitting on the bench in her all-in-one pink swimming outfit, swinging her legs back and forth

'Come on Daddy,' she said. I slapped a hand upon my forehead. I had, in all the commotion forgot that I did not have any swimming shorts. It was the last thing I would have thought to pack. I felt utterly stupid and crushed that I must now disappoint my children who sat patiently waiting and shouted aloud, 'I can't even take them swimming.' Both the children looked to the ground. I ran over and hugged them.

"I'm not angry with you,' I said holding them close.

I could rush out and buy one but that would mean walking back into town with the children and wasting my precious time with them. Although well behaved, they were beginning to annoy and elbow each other as they impatiently watched me rack my brains. I felt utterly stupid for not being prepared and after hiding in the bush, and running out of the court, it was this act of forgetfulness that broke my back.

The old lady with silver hair walked in leading the little boy by the hand. I jumped at the sight of her.

'I'm so sorry,' I pleaded, 'I did not know that this was the female changing room.'

'*Alles gut,*' she replied with a wave of her hands and began to unbutton her blouse. I gathered my children.

'There's no need to leave,' she said, 'this is the familia Zimmer.' She studied my blank expression.

'Family changing room,' she stated. 'All is good. We can all get changed together. We are all the same underneath.'

'Not exactly,' I replied. She gave a questioning half smile in return as Germans often do when trying to work out if an Englishman has just made a joke.

'I have to go anyway,' I explained. 'I have nothing to change into, not unless I go naked.' For the first time the lady spoke sternly.

'This is not a naturist place,' she said.

'No, you don't understand. I've forgotten my shorts so I can't go swimming.' This admission made both of my children groan with disappointment.

'So you have forgotten your shorts?' she repeated. The old lady gently spoke to the little boy who walked over to Sebastian and Louise and sat next to them before she disappeared from the room leaving her bag and possessions behind.

At first the little boy sat silent, until to my astonishment they all began to speak with each other. Some of children's words were in English but many in German. I marvelled at seeing foreign words coming out of my child's mouths.

'My God, you can speak some German' I said. Louise, eager to show off, answered 'Ich spreicher bi.'

The old lady returned holding out a pair of swimming trunks.

'Here,' she said, 'this is from the people that have left behind their clothes. You look similar to the same age as my son so these should fit.'

I thanked her profusely for her kindness and again was taken aback by the genuine consideration shown by a German to an outsider. She began to take her clothes off, quickly and efficiently, folding them as she did.

I busied myself with the children's backpacks looking for a towel to wrap around my waist. An apple came bouncing out and roll across the floor to a stop at the foot of the now naked lady. I sent Louise to retrieve it but the lady was already next to me with the apple in an outstretched hand. It was impossible not to admire her confidence.

A few minutes later, on the way to the pool, I passed a mirror. The Speedos I was wearing was at least one size too small.

There was an impressive number of swimming pools that could be seen at every point of the panorama when I stood with my children at the end of the entrance. A brave German, poised like an effigy of Jesus at the top of a five tier diving board, hopped into the air and shot into the water like a gannet, barely making a splash. The Englishman in me wanted to bomb next to him.

A siren split the air and like a bee hive disturbed, people hurried towards one end. My children too pulled me towards the wave pool where the water had already begun to lap against its yellow mosaic-tiled shore.

I was soon waist deep in the waves pulling a floating mattress, onto which my children clung. We bashed through the human-made surf and for a moment I forgot about England and Germany, plane flights and hotels. Instead, I listened to my children squealing with delight, their laughter washing over me like the waves.

Eventually, breathless and exhausted, I persuaded them to rest. I found an empty lounge chair by one of the shallow pools designed for smaller children. There were a few mothers holding young infants in warm water no deeper than a birdbath. I sat on the sunbed and swaddled Louise in the towel like a baby, cradled her in my arms, rubbing my nose against hers. Sebastian sat at the end of the lounge in-between my feet. He would often look back and wait for a smile or a tap of my foot for reassurance. My world was around me on a poolside chair and my heart sank at the thought that I would soon have to leave them behind.

The old lady with silver hair interrupted my thoughts and took the chair next to us. The little boy immediately walked over to the shallow waters of the infant pool. Sebastian looked back at me for an approving nod before casting his towel aside and joining him. Louise, eager not to be missing out, struggled free of her towel.

'I see they fit you,' said the lady.

Was this a German joke, I thought? I pinged at the elastic and replied with a smile. 'They are great thanks, although a little tight.'

'You are making holiday, yes?' she asked.

'I wish I was,' I replied honestly then added, more to myself. 'Then I could take my children home.'

'You are divorced, yes?' I was getting used to the German forthrightness.

'Separated, actually.' This was the first time I had used the word separated; it's less brutal and gives hope.

'No need to explain,' she said, 'it is normal here in Germany nowadays. My son is divorced. I am taking care of his son, my grandson, while he is working.' We both looked towards the children playing by the water's edge. All three, I thought, from divorced parents.

'Your children speak some German so then their mother is German?'

'Completely.' The lady looked at me quizzically. An announcement came over the loud speaker. A number of people got out of the water.

'This is for you I think,' explained the old lady. 'All the people with the blue coins have only ten minutes to leave.'

'I think I'd like to stay longer,' I answered casually.

'No, that is not allowed. You must leave. Then you can start again if you want.'

'Surely I can just pay extra at the counter on my way out?' I protested.

'No, that is strictly forbidden. You must leave now.'

I felt agitated by the rules.

'Who's running this place, the SS?'

The silver haired lady glared at me then shook her head.

'It is always sad to hear English people make jokes about such horrible things.'

I shrank under her continued gaze and felt ashamed. I apologized and thanked the lady for her help earlier yet found her answer strange.

'Why would I not help you?'

Once outside in the cold reviving air, we headed back through the town. Both Sebastian and Louise looked tired so I let them take turns riding on my back. They did not complain and I hugged them for it. The apples I'd had bought earlier at the market were a welcome treat. The smell of my children's damp hair reminded me of bath time and I felt homesick. I wished I had somewhere warm and comfortable to take them and not the hotel attic room. Every step that we took was ultimately a step back to their mother, a step closer to letting them go. I was on a conveyer belt that I could not stop, a fairground log ride.

We left from the main road and walked down a dirt pathway, which soon became lined by trees as we entered a park. This took us directly past the castle where the reflection of the witch-hat turrets and white washed walls shimmered in the surrounding moat. The ducks feeding on the pathway became scattered by Sebastian's frequent charges.

Louise clung happily to my back, only agreeing to swap her piggyback ride for a place on my shoulders. I cursed again for not having a pushchair. Other couples with children often bid me 'Güten tag' as they passed. It felt good to be considered a family again.

The pathway led to the road, and a familiar bench where people could sit and look back down across the park. I smiled at the irony when my children chose to rest at the very same bench where I had waited for their mother.

We sat for a while in silence. Sebastian turned and pointed across the road behind us. There was a building whose roof climbed slightly higher than the surrounding trees. It was facing the opposite direction so it was not possible to make out its use.

I asked Sebastian about the building but he seemed reluctant to talk. Intrigued, I picked up both Sebastian and Louise in my arms and hurried across the road. I followed a small worn pathway through the undergrowth, which continued to the front of the building. It led out into a children's play area with sand pit, slide and swings. I set them down and turned to face the front. The sign above the doors read: 'Ahrensburg Kindergarten.'

'It's a school.' Neither of them spoke and it was strange that they didn't run over to the playground. I walked to the entrance and cupped a hand against the glass door.

Hand-painted pictures hung on the walls of a brightly coloured reception area. Double doors at either end led off to what I presumed were the corridors to the classrooms. Next to these doors were coat hooks fixed in a row along the walls no higher than a metre from the ground. I remembered an early morning looking into Sebastian's classroom.

Instinctively I narrowed my eyes and read the names that were printed underneath each hook: Anselm Berger, Jañole Mülleer, and Katarina Stôtzer. I stepped back from the door realizing at once why my children had been so quiet.

'Why are your names printed under the coat hooks?'

Louise actually answered in German. 'Wir dürfen nichts sagen.'

'In English,' I shouted. Sebastian answered.

'We are not allowed to tell you that we go here to school.'

'You are already in a school?' Louise began to cry and Sebastian's bottom lip wobbled. Then, as if on cue, it started to rain.

I quickly gathered them up as the drips turned into a down pour. The nearest cover I could find was underneath the slide in the playground. I crouched down with them as we all found shelter.

It was impossible to talk over the rain beating on the metal slide. I remained silent while gently wiping the rain and the tears from their faces with the sleeve of my coat.

A low point: deep, dark, underground low. No torch to lead me out, no candle on my hat. Nothing but despair and helplessness. A foreigner in a foreign land with my children, we were wet, cold and hungry, barely sheltering from the rain. I had nowhere warm and cosy to take them, I had nowhere to change them into dry clothes, hell, it wouldn't be long before I couldn't even speak their language.

Also, I had been fooled. When I'd thought she was organising a holiday to Germany, she was booking them places in a school. I had been blind but now I could see. I felt utterly ashamed.

The rain had stopped by the time we made it back to the town but not before a few maverick rain clouds had dampened our clothes and spirits some more. The tobacconist was just closing with only a few people milling up and down the street gazing in at the different window displays. By contrast the outside tables of the bar a few properties up were beginning to fill.

I stood outside of the shop looking up to the first floor. My children stood either side of me holding my hands. I shouted up to the window.

'I'm not setting foot in there ever again so come down and collect the children!' It was a false claim anyway, as I didn't believe I would have been invited in. Surprisingly the window quickly opened and Eva called out in a kind of loud whisper: 'Don't make a scene, Richard, leave the children with my mother.'

I stared through the shop window and could see my soon to be ex-mother-in-law, puffing on a cigarette while emptying the cash register.

'I hate your mother,' I shouted and even as the words left my mouth I felt stupid at having said them. Eva spoke through gritted teeth.

'Don't make it difficult for the children.'

'*Difficult,*' I repeated the word as if it was completely foreign to me. 'I've got to leave my own children here in Germany. Now that's difficult.'

There was no answer. I looked at Sebastian and Louise. Their coat hoods were up and their timid trusting eyes looked out at me. I called again in a softer voice, which I knew Eva could still hear from the upstairs window.

'It was all planned, wasn't it?'

Again there was no answer and a hand appeared and pulled the upstairs window shut. I knelt down on the wet pavement and wrapped my arms around them and hugged them both tight. Even at that last moment it seemed incomprehensible that I would be leaving them behind. They were too young to understand but they seemed to, a little, by the way they hugged me back and looked into my eyes.

'I promise you I shall come back and get you.'

I started to cry and as I did, they cried too. I realized we looked dramatic to passers-by, a scene of goodbye that would even draw attention at an airport departure lounge. Yet that's how I wanted it. My dignity had already vanished the moment I stepped off the plane in Germany.

So in front of her mother who peered through the window of the shop, and in front of the people outside of the bar a few properties up, in front of the butchers who were clearing away their window display and the people walking by who couldn't help but stare, I wept. Also in front of Eva, who I hoped was spying through the crack in the curtains. I wanted them all to see and share the pain, the loss, the agony of letting my own children walk back into the shop and then being forced to leave Germany without them. My only act of defiance was to let them see my pain. Roll up, roll up, come see the performing daddy cry.

*

I FELL ASLEEP ON THE flight on the way back. Although there was turbulence and shudders and the continual pinging of the 'fasten seat belt' light, my chin soon pressed against my chest and I drifted into a deep stupor. I felt emotionally drained. I was fortunate in that the budget airline with which I flew had a policy of filling empty seats, whether they had been previously paid for or not, and I therefore didn't have to look upon the empty ones originally reserved for my children.

Leaving Germany did not come with a sense of relief and heading for England brought no satisfaction either. Only in the sky between, like no-mans-land in a war, did I feel strangely at ease. England was a home without my family and Germany had my family but was not my home. Thomas John Banardo, the founder of the Doctor Barnardo's Children's Charity once said that his childhood was so unhappy that he cried when he had to go to school and cried when he had to go home. I felt like that on the plane. Germany is a lovely country but it is not my country, and although England is my home, without my children it is nothing but a bare and barren land, like a body without a soul.

So perhaps unsurprisingly, I slept soundly on the flight back and only with the sudden jolt of the plane touching onto the runway did I awake. I was at first bewildered, as if I had awoken from a troubled dream.

My last memory of Germany was of the large taxi driver in the journey from Ahrensburg to the airport. He had tried in his limited English to ask questions about my trip. When talking about my children and seeing the approaching airport I had burst into tears and could not stop. The taxi driver pulled up his yellow Mercedes outside the terminal and turned his meter off. He stroked the top of my head with his fat hand as if calming a dog, and waited patiently for me to recover. He would not take a tip and I'm sure that if he could have stretched out of his seat he would have hugged me too.

Dave, on the other hand, on the other side of the flight, in my other world in England, had no such problems. Upon seeing me walk into the arrivals lounge, he shouldered through the waiting crowds and grabbed hold of me, picking me up from the ground.

'Good to see you, old mate,' he said through his bushy beard. 'What's it like in sauerkraut land?' He took my heavy suitcase under one of his arms and wrapped the other around my shoulder. 'Good to see you, old mate,' he repeated.

His rusty van was double-parked right outside the terminal in a space reserved for buses. An angry bus driver, who was trying to manoeuvre past the van, began making rude gestures at us. Dave threw my case in the back and we hurried off.

'Don't you ever get any parking tickets?' I asked, as he ground through the gears.

'I get loads,' he said, 'but the van's still registered in the name of my ex-girlfriend and she stole my TV when she left.'

It was good to smile again at such frivolous things. I felt relieved that he had not asked about my children although clearly going by the baby seat I had noticed in the back of the van, he'd been expecting them too.

Chapter 12

AFTER MUCH COAXING WITH VAGUE questions about Germany I eventually told Dave about my time in Ahrensburg. He listened intently as we drove through the country lanes, hugging the corners. As we approached a built-up area the street lamps became frequent and I could clearly see the sincere concern on his face.

'We must get your children back,' he said. I was touched that he assumed himself a part of the solution.

'Did you see much of Eva?' he asked. A vision of her walking into the court flashed into mind.

'Yes I did, but I don't want to think about her now.'

'Did she look good?' I didn't answer.

'Is she with anyone else?'

'What makes you say that?'

'Some people are like monkeys,' Dave said. 'They won't let go of one branch until they get hold of another.'

I answered sharply. 'I don't care about her, I just want my children back.'

We had reached the outskirts of Chelmsford although I did not recognise the route Dave was taking. He noticed my confusion and smiled mischievously.

'You are not the only one,' he said.

'Not the only one, what?'

The van turned sharply into a well-kept modern housing estate where all of the front gardens had hedgerows manicured to the same height. It was comforting to see familiar shaped houses again.

The exhaust of the van scraped over the speed bumps. Eventually we pulled into the car park of the Queen's Head public house, which was surprisingly full of cars for such a quiet area.

'Looks like a good turn-out,' he said, while he backed his smoking vehicle into an impossibly tight spot.

I stood for a moment outside of the opaque coloured glass pub door and stared at the blurred figures inside, hesitant to go in.

Dave held open the door. 'Ladies first.'

Our entrance was like a cowboy western film in that when the door slammed behind us, every head turned and stared in silence. They were all men, some leaning against the dark grained bar, most sat around two large tables that had been pushed together.

'This is Richard, the one I told you about.' I shot a sideways glance at Dave.

'You told them about me?'

A man stepped forward and I recalled his thin tight face and gaunt completion from outside the solicitors' office.

'I'm pleased you decided to join us. I'm Michael, the group leader.'

Dave clapped his hands together and announced, 'Who wants a drink?' I felt glad to have the attention taken away from me. I was shown by a friendly face to a seat around the table. Seeing the men joking and laughing and gulping their beer reminded me of the two German workmen in Herr Ovel's bar. I listened to the conversations and gathered by their introductory nature that some of the men were also first timers. An abrupt 'ting ting ting' of a pen tapping against a beer glass quietened the crowd before Michael made his address.

'I'd like to start this meeting by introducing our newest member.' I shrunk in my seat and shot a bolt of lightning at Dave, who grinned through his bushy beard and held his thumb up. I did not feel ready for this *I'm an alcoholic* kind of meeting. The smell of the chorine was still on my skin, and an apple core was in my coat pocket to remind me that I had spent the day with my children.

Fortunately, the eyes of the men were guided, by a sweeping hand gesture from Michael, to a small man seated on the other side of the table. He was timid looking, with deep furrows on his forehead, made all the more noticeable by his receding hairline. He, like me, did not look comfortable being there.

I began to gulp down my beer, intent on walking out; a typical bloke in that I still felt the necessity to finish my drink before leaving.

The little man spoke quietly, introducing himself as Henry, an insurance auditor from the nearby town of Witham. He bravely pushed out the words while rubbing his hands together. He seldom made eye contact with anyone. I admired his courage.

'I've got two children,' he began, 'both girls. They are my world but I'm slowly losing them. I've hardly seen them in the last month.' Everyone remained staring at Henry in silence as he swallowed hard. 'We separated about six months ago so I naturally moved out to give her some space and try and save the marriage. At first it was going okay and there was a chance we might get back together, or so I thought. But then she became difficult. When I'd go to pick my girls up at the arranged time, no one would be at the house and on other times she made excuses for me not to see them. If I argue, the girls cry and it's my fault.' Some of the men around the table exchanged knowing stares.

'I've tried to go to the solicitors, but all they do is send expensive letters at £110 a page and she doesn't reply.'

'Vultures,' somebody shouted.

'I can't afford to go to court and I'm still paying the mortgage.'

'Have you tried to get legal aid?' asked a clean-cut lad in his early twenties. Michael, the group leader took his cue. He had chosen not to be seated at the table but instead perched on a high barstool and therefore was looking down on everyone. He cleared his throat as if about to recite a rehearsed passage.

'Fathers don't get legal aid,' he stated solemnly. 'Legal aid is only awarded to those who cannot pay for it themselves; which generally means the mother as the courts will consider her the stay-at-home parent and not the bread-winner. The fathers, on the other hand, are always presumed to be the earner and long must we continue to work.' There was a jeer from around the table. 'If a father stops work,' continued Michael, 'so he can be awarded legal aid to help fight for his children then he won't have enough money to pay for his children's maintenance and the courts will take a dim view of that.'

Everyone then looked back at Henry whose cheeks flushed from the renewed attention. This time Henry spoke more quietly than before.

'Now there is another man involved,' he mumbled. The place went deathly quiet. 'And it's really making the situation difficult. Last week this man answered the door and my daughters stood behind him, like he was their Dad. I started to argue with him so the girls started crying and then he slammed the door on me. I mean, it's my door, my house, my children.' Henry swallowed hard again. 'He's even started decorating the front room,' he added. 'It doesn't even need repainting. I did it two years ago. I thought she liked the colour.'

Henry's gloomy expression was mirrored in the faces of everyone around the table. Michael broke the silence and asked a question in a gentle tone.

'Was this other man the real reason why she had you leave the house?'

'Typical,' shouted Dave.

'No, it's not like that,' insisted Henry, 'he's just a lodger.' In the silence that followed, many, like me, gave Henry a forlorn smile.

Henry then muttered something profound and it stayed with me for the entire evening. Even after the meeting had finished when other bedraggled fathers had told their stories, ranted at the injustice and promised to take action; when glasses were chinked together and pats on the back and hugs flowed as freely as the beer, I still thought upon his last comment. When at last, I had made it home and Dave's noisy van had roared off into the distance, I lay in bed in a cold empty house staring into the darkness, Henry's last comment still gnawing at me: 'I just want to get back with my wife so I can get back with my family.'

To Henry it is all linked and seemingly impossible to have one without the other. Now Henry, I thought, must start all over again; with trips to the park on Sunday afternoon and sitting in the car on rainy days and eating at McDonald's. He can't buy another house because he is still paying for the first one. He can't buy another life. His only hope of ever regaining any part of a family life is to get back with his wife. 'Of course she isn't seeing another man, Henry,' I thought. If you always deny it then there is nothing to forgive and the quicker you can get back with her. Smart move Henry, you have already worked it out.

Chapter 13

I WAS TREADING WATER, KEEPING afloat knowing that one high wave and gulp of salt water could send me to the bottom. My recent trip to Germany had drained my resources. So with gritted teeth I worked every hour that I could, keeping myself forever busy and forever exhausted, skimping and saving at every opportunity. I afforded myself little or no luxuries apart from the odd weak moments when I would point to the top shelf in Mr Patel's corner shop for a cheap bottle of port. 'Another dinner party,' he would say while tapping on his cash register.

In this way, I passed the first weeks back in England; blurry eyed and stumbling out of bed, going from one building site to the next; returning home in the dark.

Inwardly I was full of resentment and anger; profound sadness, like a dark cloud hovered over me; a raw unbandaged sensitivity.

Outwardly, I was coping well. With a facade of quiet acceptance, I armed myself with a list of phrases ready to stop any conversation that might provoke me: 'Yes, I was getting on with it' and 'Yes it would all work out in the end.' Like wallpaper over a crack, I was covering up well. At least I hoped it looked that way.

'You seem to be bearing up really well,' commented Dave one evening as he dropped me off from work. 'I haven't heard you speak of your children all day.'

'Yes', I smiled, 'I'm just getting on with it.' I waved him off then pushed open the door of my house and sat at the bottom of the stairs reading the mail. Under the pile of free papers and pizza fliers was another crisp, official water-marked envelope. I ripped it open and found the foothold on the crumbling cliff edge of which I had been clinging.

With incredulous eyes I read a letter from the Citizens Advice Bureau. It explained that if my children were to be in England, then the English courts may prevent them from leaving again until both sides of the story could be given to the court. It had something to do with a French-sounding law and if I understood it correctly, meant that both parts of the story, from the mother and the father, must to be heard before the children are allowed to leave the country. It was written in legal jargon and never committed to anything, although it hinted, using non-committal words like *perhaps* and *hopeful*, that under English law, my children should not have been taken. I remained at the bottom of the stairs, staring at the letter, the cogs of my mind turning. If I appeared in court in England, I surmised, and pretend that my children are still here, I could give my side of the story, stating on record that I do not agree to them leaving. It would at least, officially prove that I never agreed to it and perhaps help out with negotiations in Germany.

I needed something to hold onto, to help keep me afloat. I had the growing fearful realisation that I would lose Louise and Sebastian forever, that I would fade from their existence as the money for flights ran out, as they were slowly engulfed in a world that I shared no part of. I had settled in my comfortable armchair in front of the telly only days earlier to tearfully watch *Surprise, Surprise*, a television programme where long-lost relative are reunited. I had a vision of my two teenagers running across the stage into my arms while the audience applauded and wept. I had to have proof; I must be able to prove that I never wanted them to go. Yet it was going to take money I did not have.

'Exactly what do you need the loan for?' asked the young bank cashier from behind the thick glass screen. I was unprepared for such a question, as I didn't expect I would need to give a reason. The growing queue behind me of old ladies clutching cheque books and a large man on a mobility scooter was within easy earshot, and like the cashier, awaited an answer.

I noticed a poster on the wall behind her; it was of a flock of birds flying high above the English countryside. Written on the poster was the caption *The sky's the limit*. I took the birds as inspiration and stuttered my answer through the perforated holes at the bottom on the screen.

'A bird aviary,' I answered.

'A bird aviary,' she repeated with a look if disbelief. 'Just one moment.' She then disappeared through a door behind the counter. I casually stared back at the waiting line of people behind me and smiled. Bird aviary, I thought, of all the reasons to give.

A man in his early thirties with a bleach-white complexion and a tightly knotted blue tie appeared at the counter behind the glass screen.

'Mr Archer,' he began with a respectful nod. 'We are always happy to help our existing customers with loans but the bank does have strict guidelines that it must adhere to. We are not allowed to give loans without sufficient reason.' I went to speak but he quickly continued. 'If your loan was for home improvements for example that would help increase the value of your property then that would fit the criteria.' I was quick to answer.

'Well, I'm going to build the bird aviary onto the side of my house.' He tipped his head to one side.

'Does that improve your house?' he asked.

'It does if you're a bird.' We exchange a friendly stare while he searched for his next sentence. Stooping down, he spoke quietly through the holes in the screen.

'Why don't you apply for a loan to build a porch or a conservatory then once you have the money you can always change your mind.'

I waited for a moment before announcing, 'I want a loan to build a porch.' He immediately pulled out a form from underneath the counter and began to write.

'And how much of a loan would you like, sir?'

I answered clearly, 'Five thousand pounds.' The man did not look up from the form although raised his eyebrows.

'That's a big bird aviary, Mr Archer,' he whispered. After more frantic ticking, the form was slid under the counter for me to sign.

'That's five thousand pounds, repayable at eight thousand pounds over three years,' he explained. I quickly signed. The repayable fee was staggering but what did I care. Life without my family had lost its value.

The bank teller slid the form under the glass and pointed to a cross on the form. 'All we need now is your wife's signature then we can transfer the money directly into your joint account.' I was momentarily taken aback and tried to conceal my despair. I leaned down close to the perforations.

'Can I speak to you in private?'

I was expecting to be led into some quiet room or at least a hushed corridor within the inner sanctum of the bank so was rather surprised when the bank-clerk appeared on my side of the counter. He beckoned me over to the area between a rubber plant and the electronic glass entrance doors. He appeared taller this side of the counter and stooped slightly to listen.

'It's like this,' I began, and told him, more or less, of my new marital situation. I was becoming fluid with the use of words like *separated, estranged, divorce.* I didn't mention children. He listened with a fixed attentive expression. It became apparent by his practiced answer, which he easily recited from memory, that he had heard this sort of enquiry before.

'It is not possible for the bank to remove your wife's name from the account without her signing a form authorizing it, so up until then you will both,' he emphasized the word *both,* 'will both have access to the account.' I remained silent for a while. I quickly scanned his body, looked for signs that he might be a Daddy with young children: milk stains on the top of his shoulder where he may have held a burping baby, tired eyes from lack of sleep.

'She has taken my children out of the country and I need the money to get them back, hence the bird aviary.'

The electronic doors automatically opened momentarily sweeping us to one side and as if to animate the point, a young mother holding the hands of two youngsters walked in.

'I've got to get my children back, please help me.' The clerk said nothing and I wondered if he was going to call security.

'Have you got kids?' I asked. He nodded. 'And you'd do anything to get them back?'

He answered in an official loud voice. 'It is not the bank's policy to get involved in the personal matters of our customers.' Then, after a quick glance around he dipped his head towards and spoke in a hushed tone.

'Have you ever thought of setting up a personal account, Mr Archer. I will help you arrange this. Then I can see no reason why you cannot apply for a loan via that account. Will that solve your problem?' I showed open relief. Yet the bank clerk leaned even closer and added, 'And Mr Archer, if I was you I'd move all of your finances into your new personal account. You will not be the first person, husband or wife, to have their joint account plundered by the other half.'

I thanked him with a firm handshake. After a lot of form filling and extravagant signature swirls, I turned to leave.

There would be future loans to come: a conservatory, new windows and a boiler upgrade were all used as reasons to finance trips to Germany. The bank clerk, who I would later learn was called Bill, once joked that my house must look like a palace. In truth my twenty-one-year-old boiler was continually breaking down and the windows, even when tightly shut, had drafts strong enough to make the curtains flutter.

As I approached the automatic glass doors the helpful clerk called out after me. 'Good luck with the bird aviary, Mr Archer.' For that split second I have forgotten my deception so looked back with a confused expression before quickly remembering.

Chapter 14

IN THE VERY EARLY HOURS of the following Thursday I was again pacing up and down outside yet another court house, only this time it was in my own country and I merely walked ten minutes from my home to be there.

The lanes of traffic on the busy road, which lay only metres from the entrance, were filled with people sitting in their cars; some were nodding to music, others in deep morning thought. I envied their normality and did not return a smile if ever a driver's gaze met my own.

The Chelmsford courthouse was a far cry from the modern clean-cut lines of the Ahrensburg law building and did well to dampen any feeling of optimism. I had walked past this building many times and mistaken it as yet another office block, built by ostentatious architects of the 1970s; blue pastel squares underneath every window had now faded, and bulky concrete lintels were bare above the doorway. I pushed open the heavy wooden doors and entered. The floor of the entrance hall was covered in large black and white tiles and resembled a chessboard. A cleaner with a dirty rag slung over his shoulder guided a spinning floor polisher. Upon seeing me enter he whipped the electrical wire which lay across the floor and it immediately streaked out of my way like an obedient snake. I walked over and sat on one of the benches facing the different courtroom doors. I was early and the only person there. I smiled to myself: how German I had become.

I took out a letter from my inside pocket and opened the neatly folded, crisp paper; It consisted of two pages and had cost almost a day's wages to receive. It was signed with a fragmented signature from my newly appointed English solicitor, Mr Horsham, who had previously afforded me a thirty minute free consultation.

The letter had converted, into more legal expensive words, a detailed account of the conversation I had had with Mr Horsham two days earlier when I re-entered his office. He had remembered me from my first meeting and had been surprised, as he had put it, that I was *still in the game.'*

I told Mr Horsham of the advice given to me by the people of the Citizens Advice Bureau. He belittled the Bureau's abilities but when reading the letter, the lines of his forehead significantly creased as he had raised his eyebrows.

'I had heard of this approach,' he said. 'But I didn't think this would be appropriate for your situation.'

'Or fit into the free thirty minute consultation,' I said.

'It's a long shot,' he continued with his eyes briefly closed. 'Whenever a father goes up against the mother in a custody battle, it's always going to be a long shot. I think I managed to warn you of that during your *free* thirty minute consultation.' We shared a respectful stare.

'It's not exactly a custody battle though is it?'

'No, no, you are quite right,' he admitted, nodding his head which made his chin bulge against his white shirt collar. He continued to look over the letter as he spoke.

'This is what is called an 'ex parte order', parte is French for part, which effectively means you are going to give the judge half the story and then hope that the judge will not allow the children to leave this country until he hears the other half from the mother.

This, in turn, will give you enough time to show the courts that the children are settled here and how it will be detrimental for them to be taken to another country.' Mr Horsham looked up for approval. I was impressed by his knowledge. His grin was smug.

'There is one fatal floor as I see it,' Mr Horsham continued. 'It is difficult to obtain an ex parte order to legally hold children in this country when they have already been taken out.' I was quick to answer.

'Yes, but if I can just get an order from the judge for part ex parte then I can prove the children were taken unlawfully whether they are here or not and take that ruling to Germany.' Mr Horsham held the palm of his hand out as if he was stopping traffic, a gesture I'm sure he used in court.

'Stop Mr Archer, you have to disclose all of the information to the court.'

I purposely dropped an octave. 'I am aware of that Mr Horsham, but if I do not officially tell you and your barrister then you do not officially know. And besides,' I added, as passionate as a politician, 'I want my day in court. I want to stand up and tell somebody this is wrong in my language.' Mr Horsham looked quizzical at the last part of my rant.

I had finished our conversation in his office by saying, 'Now, do you want the money or not?'

I could not be sure but I thought I saw him glance at the photo on his wall of a speedboat. He then calmly detailed the financial expenses of the court proceedings to come. It was a staggering cost and my face dropped upon hearing it; an expression I felt sure Mr Horsham had seen before. I told him of the promised bank loan, which was enough to satisfy his knotted brow but he assured me that the Barrister, which would be needed in this case, would not be so understanding.

'People have a habit of not wanting to pay if they lose, Mr Archer, and this is a far from certain case. These Barrister chaps have no scruples and won't even begin proceedings without some form of guarantee or down payment. Cash will do.'

It was because of that last realisation that I buried any doubts of asking for money. I was desperate, a feeling that remained with me as I sat on the bench in an English courthouse and patiently waited while an ever-increasing number of people arrived to fill the chessboard floor. Every time the heavy wooden doors creaked I looked with growing anguish for the friendly face to arrive with the promised thousand pounds that would tide me over until the bank loan kicked in.

The gathering people milled up and down, many of them with apprehension strewn across their faces, a detail I had noted familiar to a courtroom waiting area in both countries. Those that were in conversation did so in mumbles.

The round face of Mr Horsham recognized mine as his bulk laboured across the tiles and rested on the bench next to me. He sat down with a huff and was out of breath. After a friendly greeting Mr Horsham pulled some papers from his leather suitcase.

'I just want to check some details,' he said perching a pair of glasses on the end of his nose. He recited my address and then the ages of my children. It felt strange to hear their names spoken with such indifference, as if he was merely naming the make of a car or the colour of a room. It brought home the fact that although for me, today's court hearing might potentially be the most important ever, for Mr Horsham it was just another working day.

'When is the Barrister coming?' I asked.

'Should have been here by now,' he said looking at his watch again. I began to despair and noticing this, Mr Horsham quickly added, 'But she's very good and has probably already read the brief.'

'Probably.' I allowed the word to linger prompting Mr Horsham to speak again.

'Miss Sinclair is very good at this sort of thing.'

'Does she specialize in family law?'

'Well, not exactly but she has a way of getting the judge around her little finger. It doesn't hurt to have a woman batting for your side. Besides, the judge is bound to be an old man, and a smile from an attractive lady can go a long way.' I glared at Mr Horsham.

'My God, is everything resting on a smile. What ever happened to a sound argument or even the truth?' He gave me a hard stare in return and I realise that perhaps the word *truth* was missed placed in this situation. In Germany my fate relied on Otto having a brick in the judge's wall; now a wink and a flash of teeth from my barrister was important.

Mr Horsham put the papers back into his suitcase and heaved himself to his feet.

'I'm just going to find out which court we are in,' he said before stalking off. I shuffled uncomfortably on the bench. The palms of my hands had become sweaty. I rubbed them dry on my thin nylon suit trousers.

A considerable amount of people had now gathered in the forum. At least three groups of people were crowded around a person whose legal gown distinguished them from the rest.

A loud rumble caused the forum to quieten and look towards the entrance. Someone was trying to open the door the wrong way. Dave appeared, patting plaster dust from his work clothes. His eyes scanned the room and met mine.

'I've got your money,' he shouted. Through the glass door behind him I could see his van double-parked. He walked over and we shook hands warmly and then after looking left and right he produced a brown envelope from underneath his hoody.

'It's a thousand pound exactly,' he said proudly. 'Well, it's a fiver short. I ran out of cigarettes on the way. I have been saving over a year for a new van, well, new to me, but it can wait.' I humbly accepted the brown envelope.

'Just until the bank loan kicks in,' I assured him. Then two people approaching drew Dave's attention. Mr Horsham strode up and introduced a young lady who followed close behind. She was significantly taller than him. She wore black-heeled shoes to match her dark jacket and skirt, the hemline of which finished just above the knee. The flower petal collar of the white silk blouse fluffed out around her neck and beyond the sleeves of her jacket. Her hair was light brown. She looked younger than her profession would suggest. Dave stretched out his hand.

'Hi, I'm Dave, plasterer's labourer, at your service.' She looked at him with distain. Mr Horsham made the introductions and Miss Sinclair offered a weak handshake to me. I turned to say goodbye to Dave.

'Thank you for the money, Dave, I know it took a lot to get.'

'It's just what I had hanging around,' answered Dave while looking directly at Miss Sinclair. I patted him on the back as he left, a thin cloud of dust hanging in the air.

'We haven't much time,' Mr Horsham said. 'We are up next in court number three.' He spoke in a loud whisper.

'Miss Sinclair will go ahead of us and be seated up front nearest to the judge and you and I shall sit behind, got it?' I nodded. He pulled some papers out from his case and handed them to Miss Sinclair.

'You have read them?' I asked,

'No, not yet,' she answered simply, then looking at Mr Horsham added, 'But Harry, I mean, Mr Horsham drove all the way to my office and explained the case in detail over a coffee.'

She scanned the pages as she continued speaking. 'So Mr Archer, I am led to believe that you are in fear that the mother of your two little boys may take them out of the country … to Germany, and you want the judge to hold them here until you can argue the case for them remaining with you.' She then looked up at me like a schoolteacher awaited an answer.

'Yes, I mean, no, it's a boy and a girl, but yes I want them to stay in England.'

A loud voice from behind interrupted our conversation as a court usher stepped out into the middle of the forum and announced, in cut-glass English that the courts will soon be in session. There was an immediate buzz amongst the waiting people who had already formed into individual groups. Miss Sinclair spoke in quickened pace.

'Mr Archer, does your wife take drugs?'

I was taken aback by the question. 'No,' I answered meekly.

'Is she an alcoholic? Has she ever been in trouble with the police?'

'Of course not, why on earth would you ask?'

'Can you think of any reason why she might leave with the children to Germany and not come back?' I was caught off-guard.

'She wants to go home.'

It was mitigation that hit me like a silent sledgehammer; I had just inadvertently understood Eva. Of course she wanted to go home. Where would I go if things got tough, where does anybody go?

I suddenly felt very alone, standing in a courthouse surrounded by people I did not know. My resolve wobbled. My god, I thought, am I wrong?

Miss Sinclair turned to Mr Horsham.

'I'll go ahead, Harry, and leave you to sort out the financial stuff. See you in court number two.'

'Three,' he corrected, his eyes following Miss Sinclair as she cut a line through the people. Finally Mr Horsham's attention was back on me. I had sunk back onto the bench.

'She just wanted to go home,' I said looking back up at him. 'But that doesn't mean she can take my children away. No one should have the right to do that. I'm not wrong, am I?' He waited for a few seconds before speaking.

'I hate to ask you but have you got the…' He rubbed his thumb and fingers together. I handed him the envelope; six months savings for Dave, many weeks wages for me. Mr Horsham promised a receipt.

'We better hurry,' he said. 'It wouldn't do to arrive in court after the judge.' As we walked towards the courtroom Mr Horsham shook his head.

'It's just a shame she isn't an alcoholic.'

'Miss Sinclair.'

'No, your wife. We could do with the leverage.'

I followed Mr Horsham as he pushed through the dark oak doors and into a short corridor which led to another set of doors with long narrow slit windows with thin strips of wire in them. He pressed his nose up against the reinforced glass and spied in.

'Just wanted to check where Miss Sinclair is sitting so we can get right behind her,' he said still looking through the window. His breath caused the glass to condensate.

'Now remember,' he said looking back at me. 'Once the court is in session you can only speak through me.' He looked very serious, I believe, in an attempted to ratchet up the tension. He spoke a line that came right out of an American movie and when I heard it, I realize that the photo on his office wall of him steering a speed boat, wearing a Hawaiian shirt and mirrored sunglasses, was not taken in jest.

'This is where it gets real,' he said.

'It's not Miami Vice,' I replied sharply. Mr Horsham pushed his shoulder into the door, which noisily clunked but did not move. Quickly realizing his error, he sheepishly pulled the door towards him before going inside.

As soon as the doors closed behind us there was a silence, the same silence I had remembered noticing when first entering the German courtroom. Bizarrely, I looked for Otto.

Distinct from the courtroom in Germany, the benches faced the front so that all seated would look upon the elevated seating area of the judge whose unusually large throne-like chair was positioned directly underneath the Unicorn and Lion court Crest.

I followed the backs of Mr Horsham's shiny shoes to a second row of seats. He sat directly behind Miss Sinclair and leaned into her brown hair. They spoke in a whisper even though there was no one else in the room.

'Are you all prepared,' asked Mr Horsham; he was already nodding in anticipation of the answer. She smiled confidently and turned to look at me.

'I think we have Judge Hodges, I normally do very well with him.'

Another Judge. I hoped he enjoyed his breakfast this morning and left his home with a kiss from his wife; had nothing but green traffic lights all the way to work and found a parking space easily. So much, I now understood, relied upon the mood of the judge.

Mr Horsham tapped Miss Sinclair on the shoulder, She remained looking forward.

'I've told Mr Archer that when the court is in session he can only talk to you through me.' Miss Sinclair forced a smile.

'We work very well with each other, Miss Sinclair and me,' continued Mr Horsham. 'We are becoming quite a team.' She did not answer but instead looked at her papers. The room was filled with the sound of a door handle being wiggled, which at first resembled the jangling of jailer's keys. We all looked to the door at the back of the room and automatically rose to our feet.

Judge Hodges was an unusually tall old man whose rounded shoulders, I assumed, bore the strain of years of stooping down to converse with smaller people. He walked slowly down the aisle accompanied by a female court usher who looked tiny in comparison. He shuffled past, close enough for me to smell the stale aroma of his thick tweet suit. He cast a significant shadow. I noticed that Miss Sinclair's attempts to catch his eye failed.

Judge Hodges settled in his seat and we all did the same. The usher took some papers from Miss Sinclair and handed them to the Judge who then slowly reached into his inside jacket pocket and produced a pair of glasses, which he carefully unfolded. He read in silence and I could hear the distant thumping of a road-works jackhammer. Eventually he raised his gaze towards Miss Sinclair who immediately sprang to her feet.

'If your honour will allow,' she began 'this is a simple application for an ex parte order…'

'I'll be the judge of that,' interrupted Judge Hodges ignoring the obvious pun. Miss Sinclair stuttered but quickly regained.

'And it is vital,' she continued, 'that we precede with the utmost urgency…'

'And I'll be the judge of that,' repeated Judge Hodges. I whispered into Mr Horsham's ear.

'Round her little finger, my ass.'

Miss Sinclair remained standing and began to recite the names and ages of my children, referring to them as the little boy and the darling girl… I was a kind and loving father, a dedicated family

120

man. She gestured towards me and I hoped I look significantly cow eyed although the judge remained concentrated on Miss Sinclair. She spoke of the endless nights I had stayed up when they were sick, of the full part I played as a father. It was all true, but made up, on the spot, as she had not asked me any questions. A rehearsed, passionless speech. She was good but not convincing.

'And Mr Archer,' she said gesturing towards me again, 'And Mr Archer would be devastated if my children were to be allowed to leave again.'

The Judge interrupted, looking over the rim of his glasses.

'You say *again*. Are you staying the mother and the children have already left the country?' Miss Sinclair was momentarily stunned into silence and quickly picked up a document that was lying on her seat and rapidly began to scan.

'Yes,' she stuttered, 'and we are applying for the ex parte in case they might return.'

I glared at Mr Horsham, imagining a beam of pure energy burning a hole in his forehead. I whispered loudly, 'Why isn't she telling the judge that they will definitely be coming back at some point? They are bound to come back at some point, then we can hold the children?' Mr Horsham was dumfounded. I began to whisper louder.

'I've got to tell her what to tell the Judge. There is something I want to say.' I dug into my pockets for the speech I had scribbled on a piece of paper. It was hastily written on both sides, I had stayed up late to write and practiced my speech addressing the fridge with all the passion of Shakespeare. I would finish by saying 'This is wrong, nobody has the right to take my children away.'

I began to stand up to address the judge but Mr Horsham frantically grabbed my arm and whispered.

'You can't speak directly to the Judge, it has to be this through your Barrister.' So I leaned forward to tug the sleeve of Miss Sinclair but Mr Horsham grabbed my arm again.

'You can't speak directly to your Barrister. You have to do that through me.'

'But we are all in the same room,' I protested. The noise of my voice drew every eye upon me except the judges. He remained fixed on Miss Sinclair who wriggled under his gaze. She began to repeat her *loving father* speech.

Judge Hodges swiped his glasses from his face.

'I cannot see the purpose in granting an ex parte order to retain two minors in the country if they have already left.' And with that last sentence he rose to his feet and the court usher quickly did the same. Within moments he was again shuffling past me. Mr Horsham anticipated my thoughts and laid a hand on my shoulder.

'It is not permitted to speak directly to the judge.'

*

I STAGGERED OUT OF THE courthouse as if I was drunk and veered towards two men who were standing under a sheltered area designated for smokers.

Like me, they both wore cheap nylon suits that didn't fit. I offered a nod of comradeship as I leaned up against a sand-filled concrete ashtray. One of them, a young lad of about eighteen, drew deep on his cigarette, before shaking a half empty packet of cigarettes under my nose. I declined and he gave me a confused look.

'Just lost your case, mate?' he asked.

'Does it show?' He grinned and ventured another question.

'What did you do?'

'Married a German,' I said. I gave them a brief run-down of my situation: My wife went back to her homeland of Germany with the children on holiday and never came back. They seemed more embarrassed at hearing my confession, than interested. An English trait I thought.

'And you?' I asked.

'No car insurance,' said one.

'Urinating in public,' said the other.

In the distance I saw the portly figure of Mr Horsham. He raised his arm upon seeing me and quickly plodded over.

'I don't know what to say,' he confessed.

'Miss Sinclair didn't have a clue of the situation,' I snarled. 'Her only plan was to sweet-talk the judge, which incidentally, the only person falling for that is you. Seven hundred and forty nine pounds,' I shouted.

Mr Horsham took out a cigarette and hooked it between his lips.

'It was always a long shot,' he said softly. I pushed past him, my anger rising. It was better to head for home. I walked fast, my cheap shoes tapping on the pavement. A vision on the other side of the road, an apparition; a familiar heart-warming figure of a woman pushing a child in a buggy along the leaf-covered pavements. She was mouthing something to the infant who kicked playfully. It was Helen Saunders, girlfriend of my schooldays. Her gait was carefree, striding as if she was walking on stepping-stones.

I didn't call out. What possible words could I share with her today? *Hi Helen, you look beautiful. What's that? Oh the suit. Yes, just been to court, lost the kids. Anyway how are you? Fancy a drink?*

I hurried on, breaking into a trot, towards the sanctuary of my house. I closed the door on the world then notice the red light on the answering machine flashing. I pressed the button.

At first there was nothing but a muted sound like distant voices in a tunnel. Then I recognised the voice of Eva's mother speaking to my children before the sweet sound of Louise's voice came over loud and clear.

Eva's mother, in a moment of either kindness or guilt, had allowed my children to call. Perhaps, I thought, or rather hoped, the children had been acting up and the phone call was a bribe to calm them down.

Louise spoke excitedly. 'Daddy, Oma's bought another dog,' she said. 'We have been to the park.' I then heard a bark and Sebastian gave a command in German. I bit my nails and listened intently, transfused with joy by their voices, gutted that the wicked witch of the North had bought a dog. It was another barrier between me and my children.

'I love you,' I shouted, forgetting for a moment that it was a recording. Then both the children's voices became distant again. The dog barked and Louise strained to shout over it. 'Daddy, come to my birthday party.' Then a loud beep and the answering machine cut off. Did I hear correctly, I thought, I can go to her birthday party?

Chapter 15

As I approached Tesco's car park I noticed the small crowd of men. They were holding crudely painted banners by their sides, yet to be hoisted. With a sideways glance I read the slogan 'Be fair to Fathers.' A sprinkling of children was amongst them; one man had a child in a buggy and another carried a little girl on his shoulders but apart from that, the rest were all men. Most were casually dressed in jeans and t-shirts yet some, the older ones wore neckties.

I spotted the shy figure of Henry, the timid man who had spoken with such reluctant passion at the pub meeting. He wore an anorak and a look of apprehension amongst the bantering men. As I approached he searched my features for familiarity but clearly did not recognize me.

'I was told by Michael that I should make a show of unity,' Henry said as we shook hand. 'All good men have to do for evil to exist is nothing,' he said nodding towards our group leader.

Michael did not respond to Henry's comments, although he was well within earshot. He was at the front of the crowd facing everyone with his shirtsleeves rolled up. He walked along his army like a general, pressing stickers on their chests, which read: *Dads are not just for Christmas*. Then Michael got to me.

'We must make a show of unity,' he stated.

'Where is Dave? I asked.

'He'll be here soon,' nodded Michael. 'You know Dave; he likes to make an entrance.'

It was approaching mid-morning and the car park began to fill. Some shoppers looking for a parking space shot us filthy stares as they drove passed. An angry woman mouthed what I believe were obscenities from behind her wound-up window. Unfortunately, they were directed at Henry, whose cheeks turned the colour of a ripe peach.

Looking at his watch Michael gestured for us all to gather around him. He began to count the heads and I felt like I was back at school.

'Now remember,' he began, 'when the local press gets here, don't forget to show those banners.'

'Shouldn't we have a chant?' asked one of the men at the front. Our leader looked unprepared for the question and hesitated, so the man continued. 'You know, like the hospital workers or striking miners. *We dug coal, now on dole,* that kind of thing.'

'When I worked for British rail,' began a tall man standing at the back, 'we always chanted when on picket duty.'

'It's a photographer from the local newspaper,' announced Michael. 'Not a camera crew, so it doesn't matter what we say.'

There was a loud noise coming from the entrance of the car park and everybody's head turned. The sound of the blown exhaust pipe was unmistakable.

'Look,' somebody shouted. 'It's Dave.'

His van came to a screeching halt in front of the crowd and Dave leapt out to the cheers and laughter of everyone. A few passing customers with laden shopping carts stopped and stared. Michael was momentarily stunned into silence.

Dave stood tall and faced the crowd. The women's tights he wore were many sizes too small and showed the bony contours of his knees. Knotted around his neck was a black beach towel that hung loosely down his back. He also wore black rubber gloves to resemble gauntlets combined with a cheap child's mask.

'Who on earth are you supposed to be?' questioned Michael.

Dave placed his clenched fist on either hips and lowered his voice an octave.

'I'm Batman,' he answered.

Again the crowd cheered and many passers-by in the busy car park were beginning to notice us. Michael walked closer to Dave and spoke in an angry growl.

'You don't look anything like him. Batman didn't have a beard.'

'There wasn't anything left in the hire shop,' protested Dave. 'It was either this or Dracula and we don't want to scare the kids, do we?'

A short man in a white T-shirt and trainers took everyone's attention. He had a heavy camera with a large lens that hung around his neck.

'I'm here from the *Chronicle*,' he said. 'You must be Michael.'

Dave pointed to our leader. 'No, this is Michael,' he explained, 'I'm Batman.'

A flustered Michael directed the press photographer towards the body of protesters whose banners were already held aloft. He adjusted his lens and the men began to jostle. The ex-British rail worker at the back began to chant and soon everyone joined in.

'*2 - 4 - 6 – 8, Dads do more than im-preg-nate.*'

The camera began clicking. Dave hurried into the frame. Michael, whose frustration was clearly increasing, stepped before the men and with waving hands hushing them into silence. He began to gently push the men to either side to reveal an empty parking space.

'This is why we are here,' he announced pointing towards the ground. 'This is where the fight for father's rights begins.' He pulled out an aerosol spray can from his jacket pocket.

'Look,' he said pointing to the ground. 'Where is the father?'

We all looked to the tarmac, at the painted outline of a mother and a child accompanied by the writing, *Mother and toddler parking.*

After a prompt from the photographer, Michael began to spray the outline of a stickman father on the space next to the child. Again everybody cheered and the camera clicked from many different angles.

Suddenly there was a commotion, a push, some men struggling on the floor. Two security guards had rushed over. In their attempts to grab hold of the spray can they had knocked into Michael who had fallen into the surrounding crowd. Then a kind of rugby scrum ensued, where people scrambled to hold others back or to pull yet others to their feet, only to be knocked down themselves. The press photographer expertly kept to the peripheral and captured frame after frame. Noticeably, Batman always seemed to be in the middle of it. The scuffle finished as quickly as it had started when an increased number of security men entering the fray. The police were called and most of the men, including myself, dissipated into the surrounding shoppers.

Dave and Michael stayed behind to argue with a burly female police officer who stood inches from Michael's face. Apparently, no charges could be made as the spray was only a temporary marker and could be easily brushed away.

Some hours later Dave sat at my kitchen table explaining this to me. He was sporting a grazed elbow and laddered tights.

'These are actually rather comfortable,' Dave said, pinging at the elastic around his waist.

'Suits you too,' I agreed, handing him a mug of tea. Dave gave me a warm smile.

'Sorry your court case didn't work out, mate.' I shrugged my shoulders and didn't reply.

'We showed them today though,' continued Dave searching for a positive response.

'It's pathetic,' I said quietly. 'We were protesting against not having the shared use of a parking space yet I haven't even got the right to keep my own children in this country.' Dave remained upbeat.

'It's a start,' he said, then added optimistically, 'Little acorns.'

'It's pathetic,' I repeated loudly. 'Just look at us, look at you. You're pathetic. Did you really think we could make a difference?'

Dave stopped picking at the torn knee of his tights.

'If you feel that way why don't you just go to Germany and steal them back?' My face flushed with anger.

'Do you think I haven't thought about that? My German solicitor Otto told me I could be arrested for abduction. I can't risk losing my children completely, Dave. If you actually had children yourself, you'd understand.'

I instantly regretted my last statement. Dave looked away and seemed genuinely hurt. I had forgotten for a moment that Dave was possibly the only one amongst the protestors that was there because he believed in it. Whereas the rest of us, especially me, had been forced by our situation.

In normal times I would have scoffed and laughed at the demonstration, not daring to think that one-day I might be part of them too. I had seen the look of dread on some of the fathers who walked past with arms linked with their wives, pushing children in buggies; the look of *One day soon I could be with that other race of men*. Just like the time I had overheard the two workers on the construction site.

Dave placed his empty mug on the table and stood up.

'We'll talk tomorrow,' he said, then added forlornly, 'Sorry about the court case.' As he walked towards the front door I watched his large buttocks shifting from side to side, barely contained in the tight squeeze of his ex-girlfriend's tights. I called after him.

'I'm sorry Dave. Please forgive me. You are a great friend.'

Dave turned and looked straight into my eyes. 'I'm more than that,' he replied. 'I'm Batman.'

Chapter 16

THE NIGHT TIME FERRY TERMINAL at Dover docks is a barren, wind-swept landscape if first seen though blurry eyes. After two hours of dark rainy driving, the imprints of a thousand brake lights had been burnt into my retinas.

I rolled my car to a stop in an empty car park, positioned, I hoped, at the beginning of the queue for the car ferry. I was early, a growing habit for me: I was beginning to plan ahead. The midnight ferry on the other side of a busy day, on the other side of unpredictable rush hour traffic, is difficult to calculate. I gave myself some extra time to get there, too much time; I was the first one to arrive and had no other cars to assure me that I was in the right place.

I stepped outside to stretch my aching limbs; the vague outlines of two huge cranes, like giant skeletons, looked down at me. Sea wind caused me to shiver. There is, I believe, rarely a lonelier place than an empty car park by the sea.

I got back into the car and sealed off the wind with a slam of the door. Around me, covering the front seat and strewn across the back, was everything that I might need for the journey to Germany and for my escape with the children. Unlike the plane flight, there was no requirement to purchase uncertain space.

Packing was a tearful process, sifting through what was left behind, painfully reinforced with every treasured toy found. Tiny jumpers, once pulled over their heads, reminded me that I was here, and they were there.

Yet now I was going to get them, hence the car, hence the ten-hour drive opposed to a two-hour flight, hence the children's quilts and pillows squashed into the boot, hence their night clothes that were left behind because they were too small. *I'm coming to get you,'* I muttered to myself.

One recurring memory clouded my view and sapped my optimism, a morning when, unknown to me, all was lost. Eva had walked into the kitchen while I crunched my toast. She waved a form under my nose. Of course now, when I re-play it in my mind I can see her anxious face, her overtly calm manner, her unusual carefree attitude that screams deceit with every averted gaze.

'Just until they are old enough to get their own passports,' she said, and I signed. From that point on my children were claimed as spoils in a battle un-fought, a stealthy move that I was unprepared, ignorant and too busy crunching my toast to notice. I had, quite literally, lost their nationalities over breakfast.

Within a week of realising that Eva and the children would not be returning to England I had rushed to the passport office in London with a copy of both of their birth certificates, and had their names put in my passport; a classic case of closing the door after the horse had bolted.

In a telephone conversation with Otto the previous evening, he had assured me that, by now, Eva would have organized Germany paper passports for the children. This would have been easily granted by the fact that their names appeared in her German passport. They were, in the eyes of German law, German.

Otto then asked me a question in his starkly straight Germanic way: 'So for why do you ask about the passports?'

My answer was evasive and I believe unconvincing. After I had finished with my conversation with Otto I braved another call, this time to the shop. It was after working hours so I hoped the call would go straight upstairs and be picked up by Eva or the children. Instead I heard the blank formal voice of an answering machine, installed for when the shop was closed. The beep was abrupt and I stuttered into speech.

I rushed my words. 'Hi, it's Daddy' I said with false cheer, 'I'm coming for your birthday.' And that was it. I froze and put the phone down.

I felt tired after the long drive so rested my head on the steering wheel, just for a moment. I did not want to sleep. A trick I had learnt from a lorry driver, who was often in need of a power nap, was to slump over the wheel and close your eyes yet hold the keys tightly in one hand. When you fall asleep you will drop the keys and thus be awoken, a quick power nap achieved. I rested my eyes and gripped the keys, recalling in my mind again the scene in the kitchen.

Sometime later I awoke squinting; the bright twinkling lights of a huge ferryboat completely dominated my view; a massive cast of steel and iron, the size only truly appreciated when down by the waterline in a tiny car.

Little figures dressed in high viz jackets could be seen working on the decks, with other workers at ground level waving cars into the gaping mouth. The cargo parking area looked almost full with only a few more vehicles waiting to be waved on. My heart skipped a beat. I jumped out of the car and ran to one of the workers who was using a torch to help guide the remaining cars forward.

'I'm supposed to be on that one too. Sorry I fell asleep,' I shouted, my voice competing with the wind. The worker continued directing with his torch as he spoke.

'I know you are mate,' he said. 'But you looked like you needed the sleep, so I made all the cars go around you. Don't worry. I'm going to put you on last. You'll be first off too.'

I was unprepared for such kindness and gave an inadequate *thanks* in return. The greatest proof of humanity, I now firmly believe, is an act of kindness from a stranger.

I ran back to my car to find my keys on the floor. Then with a wave of his torch, the worker signalled my car onto the rumbling gangway. He didn't even look at me as I passed.

I slept again on the sea crossing, finding a row of four seats to stretch out. Fortunately, it was calm with an easy motion to rock me to sleep; only awakened by the occasion murmur from a child.

Within a few hours, I was back in my car, turning the ignition key, feeling apprehensive yet ready. I placed a large arrow on the dashboard that I had earlier cut out of a breakfast cereal packet. When my car rumbled again over the metal gang way to the stable land beyond I immediately looked to the arrow and was reminded to drive on the right.

Ahead of me now I had just roads, roads and thoughts, a pathway forever stretching off into the distance, my children waiting at the other end. I shifted into fifth gear as soon as I could, urging the residential Belgium roads to break into a motorway. I imagined Louise and Sebastian sitting together by the upstairs window of the flat, their little heartbeats increasing with every familiar car that pulled up outside the shop. They would be drawing pictures to show me; a house with a big yellow sun and a matchstick Daddy in a car. Sebastian would already have his bag packed with dinosaurs, colouring pencils and his galactic defender Transformer. Louise would be the most eager, with the one recurring thought that would dominate everything she did and said that day, 'Daddy's coming, when will he be here?' Hope is a beautiful thing I thought, especially when heading towards it.

As the morning light began to expand, the road widened into three lanes. Within an hour of leaving Zeebrügge sea port, the signs had changed from Belgium to German and I had the autobahn to aid my progress. Dortmund, my first major destination, appeared on the road sign. Other vehicles hummed at around one hundred miles per hour yet seldom did I ventured into the outside lane. A dot would appear in my rear view mirror, then only moments later with a second glance, the mirror was filled with a Porsche that zipped by.

After Dortmund the land became so vast and flat that the tiny vehicles on the far-off ribbon seemed barely to be moving. My concentration began to wane. I took a much needed petrol break at a service station.

A consortium of engineers and architects from across Europe, I surmised, had conspired to design all motorway service stations to look, sound and smell the same. If it wasn't for the German I heard, and the *Die Welt* and *Die Tageszeitung* newspapers on sale, I could have been in any part of Europe.

I did not venture far inside. Instead, after replenishing my petrol supplies I sat outside on a grass verge supping strong black coffee from a cardboard cup. Often cars would pass with children's faces to remind me of my own. It was strange, I thought, of how easily I had adapted to an abnormal life. It wasn't so long ago that two little tooth brushes stood in a jar next to mine. Now, I was sitting on a grass verge in the middle of Germany with smelly diesel engines rushing past.

I felt tired and yearned to be normal again with a normal family life; an easy, inconspicuous, everyday routine. I wanted my old life back but the words of the poet Wordsworth rang true: *You can never go home.* I was beginning to understand why so many fathers gave up on their kids.

I continued on my journey, confined to my tin box with a bag of bitter tasting liquorice that I had bought with the coffee.

Hamburg appeared regularly in the order of place on the autobahn signboards and then, eventually, Ahrensburg lay only twenty minutes beyond. Otto Lehmann had purposely planned to work late that evening so as to be available to meet me when I arrived. I was to go straight to his office.

My excitement began to grow; it was not even five o' clock. I might actually make it to Ahrensburg before the children's bedtime. Perhaps, as a pre-birthday treat, Eva would not refuse me a goodnight kiss for them, maybe even let me tuck them in bed. I would knock on the door and be very polite and subservient. The children would hear my voice and come running.

It had been early morning light that had greeted me as I arrived on the European mainland; now, just as the sun was beginning to fade I read the illuminated road signs to Ahrensburg. I dropped a gear and drove down the tree-lined road which I recalled, having previously taken it by taxi some weeks earlier. Once again the white washed walls of the castle with its pencil sharp roofs came into view and shone like a fairy tale. It was now a familiar site and therefore welcoming.

Herr Ovel, the hotel owner, continued with this strange sense of homecoming and greeted me by using my first name as I pulled into the courtyard.

'Welcome Richard. There is someone waiting in the bar to see you.'

'To see me?' I got out of the car. I was in a hurry to run to the shop before the children's bedtime. Then I realised; it must be Eva. Her mother, 'the wicked witch of the North' would be looking after the children (teaching them spells, cooking frogs). Eva had come to negotiate, possibly now because she wouldn't want to do it during Louise's birthday party or in another expensive court hearing.

I quickly knelt down by the car door and stared into the wing mirror. My eyes were bloodshot and hair matted, there were pieces of liquorice in my teeth. I sucked and picked and swigged saliva around like mouthwash and ran fingernails through my dry and tangle hair.

Taking a deep breath, I pushed open the door. The smell of stale tobacco filled my nose. It was half empty. Three people sat on stools at the bar while other slumped on chairs around small tables. I searched for her long straight blonde hair, piercing grey blue eyes, perhaps that yellow dress. Instead I recognised the shiny bald head of Otto. He stood up from his table at the far end of the bar and held his arms out like Jesus.

'Come sit down,' he said. 'You have almost arrived on time. This is good. Our German ways are rubbing on you.'

Otto let me settle in a seat before beginning to speak. He looked intently at me.

'Whatever it is, can it wait? I'm desperate to see my children before they go to sleep. I've left a message. They will be expecting me.' Otto tipped his head to one side and reached over and gently patted me on the shoulder. I read the pity on his face and recoiled from it.

'When I lived with the Sioux Indians,' he began. Only Otto could start a conversation this way, I thought.

'When I lived with the Sioux Indians, I used to weep for my children, especially at night. The elders of the tribe taught me that if I could hold my children in my heart, then I would always be with them.'

'I don't mean to be rude,' I interrupted, rising to leave, 'but I really must hurry if I'm to see them before bedtime.'

'She does not want you to go to the apartment any more. You can still see the children but you have to arrange the time first, through her lawyer Frau Meier, and me. From now on you can't just turn up.'

I sunk back into my seat I tried to speak but my voice immediately choked. Otto spoke in a purposeful soft tone although it was as if someone had turned the volume down. I drifted in and out, swamped by shock and profound disappointment. I wanted to scream, wanted to cry, to weep as Otto did over his children in the forest.

I was supposed to be kissing my children's foreheads and pulling covers under chins, with perhaps even a gentle kiss on Eva's cheek as I walked out of the door. Fool that I was for dreaming. I remained silent, hiding my hands out of view under the table, painfully pulling my little finger back to distract me from crying.

Frau Meier had written to Otto. Eva had complained about me crying outside of the shop, with a suspicion that it may have been me in the garden late at night. Otto went to great lengths to explain how much he understood my actions, if they were my actions. He even went further to fill in the gaps when I didn't speak. He told me a little more of his own story: about his beautiful wife running off with a lesser man and how he could not bear to live without his children. So he ran away to Canada to find his soul again.

I asked about the birthday party. 'Surely not,' I cried, so loud in fact that Herr Ovel, who was now working behind the bar cleaning glasses, looked over like a school teacher.

Otto, however, remained calm and continued in his easy manner. He spoke of the positives: I could still see the children by arrangement, just for now, just until things calm down. I could still see them the day after the birthday party. We didn't want any problems before court. The pain in my little finger shot up my wrist.

'It is in the best interests for the children,' he said.

I was angry with Otto for not fighting my corner. Yet, I could not deny that he had waited out-of-work hours to talk to me in person. I knew he was a rarity in his profession. The oath he had taken to serve the people was sincerely sworn.

Knowing that I would now have to organise an unexpected day with my children, Otto made an offer.

'On Sunday your family can join with my family on a day that we can be natural,' he said. I didn't quite take his meaning but thanked him as he left the bar, his shiny head disappearing into the night. I knew him to be kind and genuine but there was something else behind his motives. He spoke only briefly of his own children that evening in the bar and when he did it was in a confessional manner, looking for my reaction and acceptance as he did.

After he had gone, after I had drunk many beers and slowly came to terms with my disappointment under the watchful eye of Herr Ovel, I recalled his story again and realised: perhaps Otto saw a little of himself in me; my struggle reminded him of his own struggle. If he could help me succeed to stay close to my family, it may in some way assuage the guilt he so obviously carried because he had not stayed by his own.

Chapter 17

I WATCHED A FLUFFY WHITE cloud drift slowly past my tiny attic window. The long drive had been exhausting and the sweaty odour of the car interior remained on my body; the smell of which induced the dream that I had been driving all night. Also, in the bar the previous night, I sat alone consuming huge amounts of alcohol. Herr Ovel had been kind enough to help me up the spiral stairs to my room where I collapse on the bed. I had again bumped my head on the low ceiling just to keep in with the air of familiarity.

I purposely missed the morning frühstück and was hoping to do the same with the day by lying in bed trying to sleep, to kill time, for it to pass in a flash, to flip a switch and have it be tomorrow, the day I could finally see my children. Today was my daughter's birthday and I remained in a hotel attic bedroom.

Eventually, I rose and paced aimlessly around the hotel. I found myself in the empty dining room reading menus that I could not comprehend. Herr Ovel walked in and looked relieved to find me.

'Perhaps you would like to help me today in making better the furniture?' he asked. I would later learn that Otto had phoned the hotel and explained my predicament.

So with growing gratitude I spent most of the day with Herr Ovel, working in the basement. His wife, a skinny lady who, like her husband wore round spectacles, walked down the steep steps balancing two cups of coffee on a wooden tray.

'You are the father of die English children?' she said. It is always difficult to understand whether Germans where asking a question or stating a fact.

'Do you know my children?' I asked. Herr Ovel was quick to explain.

'Our son goes to the same kindergarten as your children,' he said while taking a nail out of the little tin I was holding. Frau Ovel smiled and placed the coffee cup by my side.

'You have beautiful children,' she said.

A shadow flicked across the room as the shoes of a passing pedestrian clicked by the small basement window, which from outside was only ankle high. I was momently distracted. Herr Ovel and his wife took my distraction to be embarrassment and quickly changed the subject to the weather. A very British thing to do, I thought.

The day slowly passed as I spent most of my time in the basement, varnishing a small bedside cabinet in the traditional dark brown oak.

I would often listen to sharp clap-and-growl of the German conversations as people passed the basement window with only their shoes to be seen. I felt like an escaped British pilot in a safe house, or the toy maker from *Chitty Chitty Bang Bang* hiding from the child catcher. I could imagine myself as anything, anything but a father waiting to see his children and was relieved to have something to do; Otto was right in that case.

In the evening Herr Ovel offered me a free meal for my labour, which I gladly accepted. I ate this alone in a corner of the dining room after the last guests had bid me Guten arben and wandered off hand in hand. Frau Ovel brought coffee and joined me at the table. Her English was not very good and there were moments of silence while she searched for the words. She spoke to me with pity in her eyes and I felt like the last puppy in the pet shop. Frau Ovel asked about my plans for my daughter's birthday. I told her that I would be spending some of the day with Otto and then was hoping to have a small celebration with my children in the hotel bedroom. Again, she sighed and looked at me with soft wide eyes.

'It'll be fine,' I said, 'I can buy a cake at the bakery.' Frau Ovel sprung into life.

'I can make cake,' she said. I was quick to decline but she had already called out to Herr Ovel, proclaiming, I assumed, her obvious good intentions. He walked into the room drying his hands on a dishcloth.

'A cake, yes we can help, but no candles in the room,' he said. There was then a sharp interaction in German between the two before Herr Ovel corrected himself.

'Ok, candles, but be careful.'

I thanked them both and helped carry my dishes into the kitchen where the aluminium work surfaces were already clean and sparkling. Back in the bar I perched on a stool, catching bar nuts in my mouth. I had endured the day of my daughter's birthday, without my daughter, and my son.

*

THE FOLLOWING MORNING AT BREAKFAST the brown-eyed waitress beckoned me away from my dining room to a quiet recess in the corridor where a small table and a telephone stood. She pressed a button and picked up the black receiver, untangling the curling wire as she did. Before handing it over she covered the mouth piece and whispered, 'Die Frau.'

I held the receiver tight to my ear and listened at first to silence. 'Eva, is that you?'

'Hi Richard,' she said in a light airy fashion. 'You can pick up the children at nine and enjoy a lovely day with them. No need to come in the shop, they will be ready and waiting.'

She sounded up-beat and friendly. Obviously she was calling from inside the shop where people were listening, even if it was in English.

I had planned my response, I had a thousand of them; a thousand scenarios with a thousand sarcastic comebacks to make her feel small and guilty. But now, the first time I actually had her attention, I broke as if confessing to a priest.

'Oh Eva, I can't take it anymore. I can't live without them. I can't live this life without my family.'

'Ok then,' she said, still light and airy. 'When you turn up, my mother will send them out. Try not to be late and have a great day.'

'What's your mother got to do with it,' I protested. 'She doesn't get to send my children anywhere!' I waited for a response but it was too late. Eva had already hung up, or, as I suspected, disconnected the line and continued the conversation to a dead receiver for all to see. *'Oh thank you Richard, and you have a lovely day too.'*

I growled at the purring mouthpiece. 'You bloody witch.' I turned to see the big brown eyes of the waitress who I had forgotten was still standing close by. I shrugged my shoulders.

'I'm sorry,' I said, 'but my wife <u>is</u> a big witch.' The waitress stepped closer and spoke slowly for me to understand.

'Mien frau ist a grosser hexa,' she said, urging me to repeat. 'Now you say.'

I spoke the German sentence as directed and she laughed. 'You have just said in German, *my wife is a big witch*.' I committed it to memory.

*

I APPEARED OUTSIDE OF THE shop exactly on time. Louise and Sebastian squealed with delight and came running out. I got down on my knees and gathered them in, kissing, hugging, and smelling the shampoo in their hair. I did not want to linger and had already decided not to look into the shop although I could already see Eva's mother's shoes tapping at the foot of the door. This time, I had decided to give them nothing.

Otto was waiting for me in the hotel courtyard, his sparkling silver Porsche parked next to my dusty, rusty car. A small head appeared through the back window. A little girl around the same age as Sebastian waved at us as I approached, the children walking by my side.

'This is my daughter Katarina,' Otto proudly announced, 'from my second wife.'

'You have two wives?' I joked.

'No, it is not permitted in Germany.'

My children were unperturbed by the new company of Katarina and began to talk happily to her through the open door; they spoke with more German than English. Otto read the disappointment on my face and intervened.

'Today will be, speak English day'. He looked at me for my approval. 'We are lucky that the sun is shining,' he continued. 'It is a good day to be natural.'

In truth I didn't want to be with Otto and his daughter today. I would have preferred to be alone with my children and had planned to buy a little cake for Louise's birthday and together, privately, to celebrate her day in my room.

Within moments I had buckled my children into the seats in my own car and followed Otto's vehicle as it rumbled over the railway intersection. Eventually we drove along country roads. I looked back at them through the rear view mirror as they sat together; two miniature humans, rocking to the motion, both smiling back at me. They were mine, like precious jewels they twinkled, and I felt like the richest man in the world.

After about twenty minutes we slowed and turned off into a gravel driveway, eventually coming to a crunching stop in a parking area where a few other vehicles were already stationed. The children were eager to unbuckle and be set free.

'The lake,' Otto said pointing towards a forest path, 'is not far there over.'

We walked through the tall pine forest, the sun glinting into our faces from in-between the branches. The ground was soft, with a thick carpet of needles and the scent of pine increased with every footstep that disturbed the ground. Louise sat on my hip while Sebastian walked behind us with a stick in his hand. Otto had sent us ahead to follow the path to the lake while he and his daughter would organize food and then follow.

I grabbed the opportunity to be alone with my family. We looked a picture, a living portrait of members of the same clan, of ancient times, a small tribe on the move. We didn't speak for ages but wandered carefree in between the trees, trailing our hands on the rough elephant bark, warming our faces in the sun. Occasionally a bird would be startled and all three of us would follow its ascent to the sky, yet we didn't speak, not for a long time, not until a huge mass of shimmering silver water sparkled like diamonds at the base of the forest. We instinctively quickened our pace towards the lake.

I saw movement ahead. I looked in disbelief and squinted to focus again. A couple approached holding hands, and I stopped. Louise took no notice although Sebastian cheeks slightly reddened as he hid behind my leg.

'Güten tag,' they said as they passed. 'Guten tag,' I replied with an embarrassed smile. My gaze followed them both as they walked up the forest pathway, their bare buttocks shifting up and down in unison. Then a splash from the lake; a man balancing on the end of a log that protruding out over the water and a woman swimming, calling for him to follow. They were both, like the couple that had just passed, completely devoid of clothes, naked and free for all to see. Now, I understood what Otto meant when he said to be natural. I had naively walked into a nudist camp.

I heard Otto calling and I turned to see him strutting towards us. Predictably, he seemed completely unabashed, wearing only his sandals and a backpack. He shuffled through the pine needles, holding Katarina's hand, who was wearing a t shirt. He did not mention his nudity and picked out a spot to lay a blanket and began placing the plastic food container and thermos full of coffee.

'Come sit and eat,' he said, 'it is a beautiful day to be natural.'

I wanted to remind him that I came from England, where it is not natural to be natural. We all sat on the tablecloth and Otto passed sandwiches while I filled the children's cups with orange. I managed to strategically place the thermos flask to inhibit my view of Otto's lower half.

I found the situation awkward but then all of my situations lately had been awkward. The conversation between Otto and myself was different this time. With our children present we both skirted around my predicament. Otto told us of his hiking holiday in Scotland where it was too cold to be natural, and I told him about my workmate Dave with his bushy beard and terrible driving. Eventually though, like a magnet, our conversation homed back to the situation that had brought us both together.

'The Sioux Indians taught me to hold my children in my heart,' he said holding a clenched fist to his bare chest. 'Then you will never be without them.' He allowed the thought to linger. Of course I agreed, but what else was I to say. It wasn't the kind of statement I heard everyday on a British building site. Dave would never say such a thing. Dave would never say it naked.

A large lady wearing only sandals shuffled by and bid us Güten tag. Nobody looked, nobody stared and nobody cared.

When everyone had eaten, the kids began to play together by the water's edge, shrieking with laughter. Otto stretched out to sunbath, thankfully choosing to tan his back.

I took the opportunity to wander. I found a small clearing in between the bulrushes where the lake gently lapped the shore. It was out of view from everyone. I slipped off my clothes, removing the last article with some trepidation. I had a strange feeling of liberation as I slowly walked into the water; the cold around my middle reminded me that I was indeed swimming naked in a German lake. As soon as I was out, I put my shorts back on.

We all stayed by the water for a few hours, eating and drinking, until eventually I had to bid Otto and Katerina goodbye. I was desperate to get back to the hotel to celebrate Louise's birthday, just the three of us, before their inevitable return to Eva and the wicked witch of the North.

'Don't stand up,' I said to Otto, 'I'll just say goodbye now and I'll see you outside the courthouse tomorrow morning.' I then added jokingly as we walked away, 'And don't forget to wear some clothes.'

Otto replied flatly. 'Yes, for sure, it is not permitted to be natural in the court.'

It took over an hour for me to find my way back and pull into the hotel courtyard. The children were sound asleep in the back, leaning against each other, their chests gently moving up and down. I stared at them for a moment before waking them.

'I have a rabbit!' said Louise as she jumped out of the car, her eyes blinking in the light.

'For my birthday, a rabbit,' she repeated.

'With big ears,' added Sebastian.

'A rabbit, a dog,' I grumbled. 'What else will your mother buy you to keep you here.' I then added, somewhat pathetically, 'We can buy a rabbit in England too.'

I led both of my children by the hand across the courtyard. The waitress stood at the entrance to the spiral staircase. Her smile was beaming.

'Alles Gute zum Geburtstag,' she said to Louise, who danced under the attention. The waitress leaned upon my shoulder and whispered. I could feel her breath on my ear.

'Your room is ready.' I presumed she meant it had been cleaned since this morning so I thanked her. Our eyes fixed on each other for longer than was necessary.

Carrying Louise and guiding Sebastian by the hand, we all climbed the spiral staircase, our footsteps echoing as they slapped against the worn marble.

Panting for breath we reached the top. Both Louise and Sebastian simultaneously notice the sign and became enthused with excitement. My door had been decorated with ribbons and glitter and a large hand written sign which read: *Happy Birthday Louise*.

The inside of the room had been completely decorated too with tassels strung across the ceiling and an Alles Geburtstag banner pinned across the wall; ribbons had been tied on the knobs of the cupboard and draped over the photo print of the castle. On the small bedside cabinet was a chocolate cake, and some small candles. I noticed with a smile that next to the cake was a box of matches that I felt sure Frau Ovel had added in defiance of her husband.

Sebastian and Louise jumped around the room as if electrified. Two small presents wrapped and placed upon the bed were quickly ripped open; both had a marzipan strip and a kinder egg. I rummaged through my suitcase and pulled out the two carrier bags full presents I had brought from England. As well as a Postman Pat figurine for Sebastian, I had selected presents for both of them that would help keep me in mind: pencils with *Made in England* on the side; a pencil case with the British flag, a 'Daddy's girl' t-shirt although I doubt if she would be allowed to wear it. I was beginning to play the game.

Sebastian and I sang happy birthday to Louise and after the candles had been blown out with a theatrical huff I watched the smoke drift out through the attic window. We munched our way through the chocolate cake including the icing before I quickly guided them to the top floor bathroom to clean their hands. For the last hour I laid on the bed and watch Sebastian and Louise fill in colouring books that were spread across the floor. It was as if we were in the front room of our home.

Later, I dropped the children off at the back door of the shop and my heart sank as I watched them run up the stairs to the voice of their mother. I did not go back to the hotel bar for a drink although it looked crowded inside, full of happy laughing people, their enlarged silhouettes dancing on the tobacco stained windows. I wanted to thank Frau and Herr Ovel and also the waitress for their kindness. But I feared the inevitable pity I would receive in front of a bar full of people; heads dipping to one side as they relayed my story to others. So I opted for my attic room and lay on my bed listening to the passing trains, wondering if the children were listening to them too.

Chapter 18

THE YOUNG RECEPTIONIST WITH AUBURN hair greeted me as I entered Otto's office. I remembered her from my first visit. She gave me a smile of recognition from behind the reception counter before walking around to my side and offering a weak handshake with a slight bow of the head. She directed me over to a small room in the inner sanctum of the office. This space was more of a partitioned-off area than an actual separate office room. The tightly stretched canvass walls wobbled when the door opened. There were no windows to the outside world and the only natural light came from the obscure glass above the door. The room was sparsely furnished with a single office table surrounded by plastic coated chairs. A water dispenser stood alone in the corner, occasionally omitting bubbles.

The secretary flicked her auburn hair from her face before gently closing the door. I sat alone at the head of the table. There was nothing in the room to distract a person's thoughts from any intense conversations taking place across the table; a purpose-built piece of German planning, I supposed.

'The business in the courtroom,' Otto had said while being natural in the forest, 'is only to make legal what we agree in the conference room. The conference room is where it all happens. Don't worry, the conference negotiations room will be in English.'

'What if we don't agree?' was my obvious response. Otto had skirted around the subject. He spoke of the need to compromise and explained that in these cases there were seldom any winners, reminding me, always with a stern look, that we had little or nothing to bargain with.

Yet I did not need to bargain because this time I had a car in the courtyard of Hotel No6. I had already packed my things in the boot and purposely reversed it into the courtyard so it would be facing out for a quick exit. A bald head appeared around the door. Otto looked worried and hastily ushered me up from my seat.

'Come bitte,' he said, 'into my office, we don't want to be the first ones here. We mustn't look eager.'

He hurried me out of the room and gently pushed a hand into the small of my back to speed me into his office. I was left there alone. In seconds I could hear the unmistakable voice of Eva, accompanied by her legal advisory, entering the office suite. My heart thumped.

I pressed my ear upon the cold dark vanished door and listen to my wife's voice. Her tone was high and pleasant, polite and formal. I paced like a caged tiger until Otto pushed into his office again.

'Do you remember what I taught you about the Sioux Indians,' he said. I made a quick Y pushing my forearms together and splayed hands.

'That is good. You are at another fork in the road.' I waited for another oration, more perhaps about the Sioux Indians but within moments he was straightening his clothes and beckoning me to follow.

'We have kept them waiting enough,' he said.

Eva and Frau Meier were seated on one side of the table; Otto shook hands, first with Frau Meier and then with Eva. I nervously misjudged the distance and squeeze the end of her Frau Meier's fingers. Her eyes glared at me from within the thick surrounding mascara. Eva and I did not attempt such formalities. Both Otto and Frau Meier looked at our reaction towards each other. We smiled cordially. Under the artificial light Eva looked tired and drawn, the creases in the apex of her eyes appeared deeper and she wore more make up than usual. Close up, Frau Meier looked ten years older than I had first thought. She was covered with fake tan and gave forced smiles with tobacco stained teeth.

For a few long drawn out seconds there was silence. Both Otto and Frau Meier shuffled and tapped the papers in front of them, neither seemed willing to speak first. In a nervous impulse I looked at Eva and made a joke.

'Who's your friend,' I said nodding towards Frau Meier. 'Is she single?' My humour was lost on Otto and Frau Meier who looked perplexed although I was sure Eva was forcing her lips to stay straight. Surprisingly she spoke first.

'Did you enjoy your time with the children?' she said. I could not immediately judge whether the question was sincere or sarcastic.

'Yes, thank you,' I replied. 'I had a very natural time in what little time we had. I hear you bought Louise a rabbit. Strange you were always against pets in England.' Eva gave a smile that never got as far as her eyes.

'It was you that suggested that my mother buy another dog.' Her comment cut deep and I curled my toes up in my shoes. I looked to Otto for support.

'I'm sorry to have kept you waiting,' began Otto addressing Frau Meier, 'but Mr Archer and I had a few last details to go over. We are feeling very generous.'

'Good,' replied Frau Meier without missing a beat. 'You will need to be.'

Otto, to his credit, remained unfazed and reached for a piece of paper from inside his jacket pocket and laid it flat on the table. There was a list typed upon it which I did not recall making with him. Otto began to read.

'It is in the best interests of the children,' he began, speaking more to Frau Meier than to Eva. 'It is in the best interests of the children that the father maintains full access to the children.' He theatrically nodded to Frau Meier in an attempt, I believe, to get her to instinctively copy. She did not.

'Every child needs a father,' he said. I suddenly realized that my access to the children was up for debate. I had naturally assumed, up until then, that I would always be getting it.

Frau Meier pulled out her own list from within her leather suitcase. It was somewhat longer than ours. I looked at Eva. She seemed as perplexed and unprepared to see the list as I was. Frau Meier flattened the piece of paper on the desk and for the first time I noticed that her nails were long like eagle's talons, and painted red.

'Finanzen,' she said before quickly swapping into English, 'Finance. Before we can speak about access to the children, there is money to be paid. Since the whole time my client has been in Germany, Herr Archer has sent no monies for the children. We can talk of nothing else until this is settled.'

My face flushed, my mouth became dry. I had just spent all my money just to be there. Otto strained his neck to read Frau Meier's list. She made no attempt to turn the paper towards him.

'This is too much for back-pay,' he said. 'A monthly amount yes, but no back-pay.'

I found my voice. 'You can't take my children to another country then tell me it's my fault that you have no money. If you can't afford to keep them here, then give them back to me.'

153

Eva spoke to Frau Meier in German. I slammed my hand on the desk.

'English please.'

There was a moment of silence, and Otto shot me a glare of pure lightning. Frau Meier looked at Otto.

'This explains a lot,' she said.

I gave an embarrassed smile and tried to look submissive although my blood was boiling.

'My client is eager to pay for his children but please understand he is sad and...' I quickly interrupted Otto.

'I want to take the children back home, Eva. This is madness, I want to take them home.'

'They *are* home Richard, my home and I need money for them.' It was the first civilly spoken sentence we had shared since she left England.

'Can I see them this afternoon, after school?' I asked. Her eyes widened when I used the word school.

'Yes, of course, but I need money.'

'And can I take them back to England for a holiday?'

'No, Richard, that would only confuse them.' I stood up from the table. Eva rolled her eyes yet Frau Meier feigned surprise.

'I can't stay here, Otto,' I said, 'This is all wrong and it's making me feel dizzy.' It was true, my head was spinning. 'Please act on my behalf,' I said touching Otto on the shoulder. Both Eva and Frau Meier gave each other a perplexed stare but said nothing.

When I reached the door I looked back and said, 'I haven't even got the right to be included on a supermarket family parking space.'

The receptionist with auburn hair smiled at me as I passed, which I found profoundly comforting. Otto hastily followed and held onto the main office door before it closed behind me.

'I shall argue for you a good arrangement to see your children. What ever it takes,' he said.

'I'm running out of money, Otto,' I confessed.

'Fear not, my English Friend' he said. 'I am Robin Hood and shall take from the rich and give to the poor.' I felt confused that in my hour of desperation Otto seemed so upbeat. He appeared mischievous, like a child.

'I'll see you this afternoon in court,' he said. 'And please my friend do not be desperate.'

Chapter 19

OTTO ROSE FROM THE TABLE outside of the coffee shop as I approached. He had been patiently waiting, knowing my route to the court would take me past.

He slurped the last dregs and placed the cup down.

'Come,' he said, 'we can walk to the courthouse together.'

It had been two hours since I had crashed out of the conference room and headed back to Hotel No6. My little attic room had been spotlessly cleaned and my suit lay out on the bed. A small bread roll had been wrapped in a serviette and placed on the bedside cabinet.

I decided not to dress formally and instead wore jeans, my traveling clothes; a small demonstration on my part of my contempt for the people I was supposed to be impressing.

'You do not wear your suit?' asked Otto as we strolled up the narrow street to the courthouse.

'Will it make a difference?'

'Yes, for sure,' he answered. 'You must always work to impress the judge and show that you are a respectful father.'

'If I wear a suit, will the judge let me take my children back to England?'

We turned a corner that led to the now familiar paved courtyard outside of the courthouse. The revolving doors were already rotating with solemn, smartly dressed people. Otto touched my elbow as we entered the marble forum and spoke softly.

'How do you say it in English, *Keep your chin high.*'

'Up,' I corrected.

'Yes, for sure, keep your chin high up.' We entered the elevator together.

'I have argued a good deal for you,' he said, 'and better still, we have Judge Heinrich. Remember I told you I have a brick in her wall.'

We were assigned to a different courtroom on the first floor. Once inside, it looked remarkably similar to the last one, with clinical sparseness and bare white walls reflecting the neon light.

Eva and Frau Meier had only just arrived when Otto and I walked into the courtroom. We all settled behind a dark oak table opposite each other. Everyone exchanged respectful stares except me. Like Perseus to Medusa, I resisted eye contact with Frau Meier.

Before any of us could comfortably settle into our chairs Judge Heinrich entered and we rose to our feet. She was young for a judge, around forty with short brown hair. Compared to the slow laboured shuffle of most Judges, she positively skipped into her seat at the head of the table. Her court aid, a frail woman by comparison and many years her senior, scurried to keep up. The judge looked directly over to me and then to Eva as she sat down. I was impressed by the obviousness of her actions.

Otto whispered to me that most of the court proceedings would be in German as so much had already been decided in the conference room. 'It is purely procedure,' he said and promised to talk me through it.

While Judge Heinrich read through some documents with her advisor, Otto spoke excitedly about the Judge; how she had grown up in Soviet-controlled East Germany and like Otto, had been separated from family by the wall.

'That's why I have a brick in her wall,' explained Otto. 'Her English is not so good but she speaks Russian perfectly. Do you speak any Russian?' he added.

'I'm English.'

'You make a joke, Yes, this is very good but now I must quickly tell you of the agreements I have made for you.'

I looked across the room. Eva and Frau Meier were deep in whispered conversation. Otto drew closer to me.

'I have secured the right for you to see your children,' he announced triumphantly. I mocked enthusiasm.

'Do you mean to say I can see my own children?'

'Yes, whenever you want, whenever it is practical that is.' I was relieved that Otto had mistaken my sarcasm for sincerity.

'And to England?' I asked. My tone was now genuine and pronounced the word *England* loud enough for all to hear.

Otto fidgeted in his seat then whispered so faintly that I had to move significantly closer to hear him.

'Do you trust me?' he asked. I nodded automatically. 'Then please be your English self. Soon, I will have a declaration to show you.'

'Can I see it now?' I asked.

'Now is not the time.'

'What if I don't like it?'

'Then you must follow that fork in the road. Be your English self.'

It was an unusual expression for Otto to use and I had not heard it before. Otto shot a sideways glance at me and studied my reaction to his request. Had Otto, I thought, suddenly become unsure of himself? He looked nervous. The court usher purposely cleared her throat and we all looked to the front.

For the next few minutes I was a spectator. The conversation led by Judge Heinrich was conducted in German. It was a strange feeling, akin to a child in a room full of adults. Occasionally everyone would look at me followed by a prompt from Otto to answer either *yes* or *no,* questions about my profession or place of birth. Otto quickly translated as best he could. I studied their faces. Everyone seemed polite and formal with no trace of malice attached to their responses, even Eva spoke without the usual quiver in her voice. Then, like a temperature drop, the mood changed. Frau Meier produced a piece of paper. Everybody looked sternly at me. It was a two-page document that seemed identical to the one that Judge Heinrich first held before her.

Otto read aloud and I realized why he had grabbed the seat to my left because now he was facing the judge who without a great knowledge of the English language would, like me, be concentrating on his facial expression.

'This is the document that your wife's lawyers have prepared for you.' He picked up the document and held it aloft like Neville Chamberlin.

'They have agreed to let you see the children whenever you come to Germany and when it is practical to do so.' Otto paused to swallow although I believe he was really giving time for the court usher to translate for the judge.

'On the condition that you sign this declaration.' Otto slid a document in front of me again and said, 'I have prepared one for you in English. Please read it and sign if you will.'

His eyes then bored into me along with Eva, Frau Meier, and the Judge and her assistant. In the silence I could hear my own heart beating. Otto produced a pen from his inside pocket and placed it precisely horizontally to the paper.

I read the first line: *I Richard Archer agree to meet all of the financial obligations expected by German law for the welfare of German children.*

My reaction was instantaneous and it came straight from my gut. With narrowed eyes I looked across the table at Eva who shrunk under my gaze. I placed a flat palm on the document on the table and pushed it away from me. I turned to Otto.

'Could you please translate my words to the Judge?' I asked.

I then spoke as if firing from the hip. It wasn't an organized speech or rehearsed yet it flowed as if I had been practicing for months; a whirlwind of emotions that came out in order.

'Who are you?' I began looking directly at the judge. 'Who are you?' I repeated this time looking at Frau Meier. 'Who are any of you to tell me what I should do with my own children. Two months ago I was ignorant to the existence of most of you. Now I must satisfy this court so I can see my own children. Never. They are not your children. They are not German, they are my children and I will sign nothing to satisfy you.'

Otto had been rapidly translating my words to the judge with an expert ability; his volume never being higher than mine and his German sentences always finishing before my new ones begun. Also he did not argue my words, as I thought he might do; in fact there was a distinct look of admiration on his face. I waited for Otto to translate my last sentence before dramatically, slowly pushing the document off the table so that it swayed back and forth like a feather before resting on the floor.

Chapter 20

I SAT ON THE SWING in the small playground outside of the Kindergarten watching the world sway back and forth. A few parents, all of them mothers, had begun to gather outside of the entrance of the school. Some were rocking pushchairs and others running fingers through their hair as they spoke. Often one of them would afford me a quizzical glance.

A woman's voice called out my name. I squinted and recognised the round spectacles of Frau Ovel. I met her half-way across the tarmac road.

'You have come to collect your children?' she said with a smile.

'Yes, I am allowed,' I stated. 'I know I am early but I need to get my children quickly. It is the last day so I want to make the most of it. Can you help?' Frau Ovel showed the same genuine concern, as did her husband.

'For sure I can help,' she offered. 'I will ask the teachers for you.'

I blessed my good fortune for meeting Frau Oval and followed her through the doors of the kindergarten. The eyes of the waiting mothers followed us both. Inside the school, the smell of floor polish and disinfectant filled my nostrils as we walked up to the main desk. Frau Ovel spoke to a young receptionist who looked at me while Frau Ovel explained my situation. The receptionist said 'No problem' in perfect English. I asked her if she had ever lived in England. I thought it better to control the conversation.

'In London for many years,' she said as she walked around to my side of the counter.

'If you wait here I'll bring your children to you. Their lesson is nearly over so it won't be a problem for them to leave early, just this once.'

As I waited I tried to look casual, leaning up against the reception desk chatting to Frau Ovel. We looked at the painted pictures that lined the walls. She showed me the one that her son had completed, of a stick man and woman, both with round spectacles.

Then I heard a familiar squeal of delight. Louise came running and dived into my arms. I swung her around like a fairground ride. Sebastian came running too then slowed for the last metre so I could go to him. I had them both in my arms again.

I thanked Frau Ovel and had a sudden flash of guilt for my deception. I picked up the children's bags and quickly left the building.

Other parents were turning up, mothers congregating in groups of four. Sebastian spoke in English as we walked outside, which attracted much attention. I remembered the pathway, which led around the back of the Kindergarten to the park. I hurried my children through the groups of mothers some frowning, some smiling, all of them looking.

We made it to the pathway yet before we could disappear into the tree, a voice called out. I turned. It was Frau Ovel smiling, jogging towards us. She handed Sebastian a painting he had obviously completed that day. I thanked her but as I looked over her shoulders a familiar unwelcome figure came walking towards the school. Louise spoke her name; fortunately she said it in

English: *Grandma*. Louise looked at me in horror and I wondered for a moment if she knew what was happening.

I bid a final farewell to Frau Ovel before turning and hurrying along the path, skipping over roots and crunching across fallen twigs until eventually the stark white castle could be seen on the other side of the road. I continued to trot as fast as I could, my arms burning from holding Louise in one and pulling Sebastian with the other. We scurried alongside the road. I wanted to turn a corner that would put us out of immediate view.

I thought of my Uncle, a sudden flash of his story came into my head. He had escaped from a German prison camp and stolen a farmer's coat to disguise his uniform. When he walked past a sentry he had to hold his nerve and not look back until he could turn a corner. Strange that so many years later I would be doing the same thing with my children.

Sebastian began to complain; his little legs were trying to keep up. I pulled him along while he desperately held onto his painting. We finally turned a corner and rested against a wall. I crouched down so we could catch our breath.

'Do you want to go home to England?' Sebastian's face lit up but to my surprise Louise initial happiness soon turned to a frown.

'Can we bring the rabbit too?' she asked.

Yes, of course, the rabbit, I thought, the stealth move; the ace card that Eva had played. The permanent bond to German soil.

'I'll buy you another one in England,' I said even though I knew how pathetic it sounded.

We continued on through the streets of Ahrensburg; desperately swapping from running to walking to resting to running again; past the expensive hotel, past the cafes with the tall tables outside, through the square in the middle of town, past old men who *tut tuted* as our shadows interrupted their game of chess.

We continuing on down the cobbled path that was covered in newly shed leaves, the sun twinkling between the buildings.

Eventually, we turned into the alleyway leading to the hotel courtyard. I had soon buckled the children into their car seats. My heart was thumping, excited and scared. I was taking control; I was taking my children back to England.

I had imagined that my children would be cheering at this, screaming with joy. But one of them was crying. I could see Louise in the rear view mirror, her eyes red and anxious as the car pulled away.

'I don't want another rabbit,' she cried.

I tried to ignore it and to concentrate on the road as the car rumbled over the cobbles but I am a weak and feeble man. I joined the queue of waiting cars at the railway crossing as Louise's continuing cries cut into me. I felt sure that Sebastian's emotions would soon follow. I rattled the gear stick and swore aloud. Begrudgingly I pulled the car out of the line again and headed back the way we had come.

The service road behind the tobacconist shop was narrow and hard to navigate. Rubbish bins and bottle crates slowed my progress. I pulled up alongside the bush I had once hidden in.

'Where is the rabbit?' I asked.

Louise immediately stopped her whimpering and wriggled to be loose. I pressed both release buttons of the children's seat belts. As soon as I opened the rear doors Louise was outside of the car and Sebastian followed, still clutching his painting. I creaked open the unlocked back gate. Of course there was a gate I thought, a simple fact I had missed the night I choose to vault the fence in my escape.

I had not yet decided what I was going to do. Abducting a rabbit was not in my plans; to stow it away along with my children on the ferryboat crossing to English.

I tip toed down the garden pathway but the children, forgetting to be quiet, ran ahead. They stopped at a sack-covered box that was positioned below the window.

Eva, I hoped, would still be in the courthouse or in Frau Shultz's office, reading forms and signing away my rights to the children. And her mother, who Louise had seen arrive at the kindergarten, would still be at the school waiting, complaining, waving her wand.

Both Louise and Sebastian proudly pulled back a cover over the rabbit hutch. A brown ball of fur scampered. It was huge. With drooping ears and a twitching nose. It took up a third of its living space.

'Look at the size of it,' I said. 'Why couldn't you have a gerbil?'

Louise slipped a finger throw the wire mess and stroked its fur.

'Can we get it out and play with it?' pleaded Louise.

I stepped back a few paces and rested between two flowerpots on a low retaining wall. My children called out to me but I was somewhere else, almost numb, lost to another world. I looked at them as if they were not my own, as if they had somehow pulled away from me. I was in the audience of a cinema watching a movie, watching my children vying for the attention of the rabbit. They both ran back to the patchy lawn and pulled up clumps of grass to poke through the wire mesh.

I heard voices from the side alleyway that led from the front of the shop, then the screech of the gate. Both my children ran into the legs of their mother. I did not look up and remained seated on the low brick wall. There were words spoken, loud angry sentences. I could hear them but did not comprehend. Eva was standing over me. I could see the hem of her dress and her lace-up brown shoes that were scuffed at the toes. I felt a little hand on top of my head and heard Sebastian's soft voice. My throat filled with emotion and I swallowed hard. I fixed my view onto the ground and walked out via the creaking gate and into the street in front of the shop. Some people were passing; a couple strolling hand in hand.

I started to run, crossing the road without looking; a beeping car rushing past me with only inches to spare. I did not care; the anger inside me converted into energy and I pumped my legs to drain its force. I ran on the road to avoid the orderly pedestrians on the pavements, haring past for all to see. I slipped on a greasy drain cover and almost lost my footing and grabbed hold of a lamppost to regain my balance before continuing again. My lungs were heaving and my throat was burning. Mothers pushing prams stopped and stared as I ran passed. I looked up to see an office worker gaze down from the high-rise buildings while stirring a cup of coffee with a pen. I saw a motorist peer into his rear view mirrors after he passed.

I ran on through the streets full of shops and out into the industrial part of town where there were less people. Eventually my engine slowed and I came to rest, panting like a dog, against a large brick wall of a multi-storey car park. I caught my breath and climbed the concrete staircase, my echoing footsteps bouncing off the hard walls. And then at the top, a flash of light, the bright sun burnt into my eyes as I opened the door. I was momentarily blinded and stumbled out onto the rooftop parking area and only stopped when I reached the surrounding concrete wall.

The wind blew into my face as I looked over the edge, the sudden rush of air causing a sharp in-take of breath. My view was of the west side of Ahrensburg. The toy town houses with its steep roofs followed the curves of the tree lined cobbled streets. From high up it looked peaceful like a model railway town.

The railway tracks cut a line through the heart of Ahrensburg, most of the shops and apartments situated on either side. Somewhere there stood my hotel, but I couldn't see it hidden behind other buildings. Yet I could easily make out the railway crossing; I followed it to the street of the tobacconist. I could just make out the place where I had stood crying with the children on that rainy day. Now little miniature people walked passed the shop like ants. They might even be my children.

My heart ached to think of that day, the day of the first realization that they were not coming back. Everything since then seemed pointless; a waste of heartbeats and hope. I shook my head and spoke out loud, my voice carried off into the wind like an autumn leaf; 'They are never going to let me take my children home.'

In a rush of imagination I flicked through the photos of my children in England, in an English life that I had intended: school uniforms, playing conkers in the park, homework in front of the telly; being called in from the garden for tea.

I looked again over the parapet, my face staring straight down at the small squares of paving slabs. I allowed a blob of saliva to drop from my mouth and fall straight and true.

Suddenly a voice spoke in German. I turned to see a man of about thirty with long scraggly hippy-like hair. He was scruffily dressed, at least by German standards; he wore a blue denim shirt that hung loose about his waist with buttons both at the top and the bottom undone. His jeans, like the shirt were faded. Most notably of all he wore socks underneath his open toe leather sandals.

Again he spoke in German, this time with sympathy in his eyes.

'I'm sorry, I don't speak much German' I explained. The man looked greatly relieved and swapped to English.

'Would you like to talk about it?' he said.

'Talk about what?'

He nodded tentatively towards the view beyond the outside wall.

'Come away from the edge,' he said softly, 'and we can talk about it. It's never as bad as you think it is.' I was confused by his statement but quickly retaliated.

'How would you know how bad it is?'

'I was once where you are. It's never as bad as you think.' The man then braved a smile and stepped a little closer.

'Come away from the edge. Let's talk. Nothing will be solved by jumping.'

I was momentarily stunned.

'Did you think I was going to… is this a joke.' I laughed although he did not seem convinced. I leaned back resting a hand on the top of the wall. The hippy man lunged forward, his scraggly hair flaring in the wind.

'Nien,' he screamed, 'Tue es nicht.'

He grabbed hold of my arm with both of his hands. I was shocked by the sudden physical contact and gave a typical British reaction of half embarrassment and half joking.

'Get off, you smelly German. I'm not going to jump.' I wriggled free and stepped to the inside of the parking area leaving the German between the outer wall and myself.

'I was never going to jump!' I shouted. 'I just wanted to see the view.'

There was a stand-off while I straightened my clothes and he guarded the outer wall. He spoke again, this time in a somewhat calmer, practised manner.

'Let's walk down the stairs together,' he suggested. 'We can talk as we walk to the bottom. It's safer that way.'

'It's quicker if we jump,' I joked, but the man's face looked stricken, so I headed to the doorway of the stairs while being closely followed by my new sandal-wearing friend.

'I was never going to jump,' I repeated as we descended down to the ground level.

He stayed with me for some of the way back, telling me more of his own story than listening to mine. His mother had passed away while he was still at school and his father left many years before that.

'I was all alone and like you, I wanted to jump too,' he said, looking for my reaction. 'Yes, I was going to jump,' he repeated, 'but then I found Jesus.'

'You found Jesus in the multi-storey car park?'

'I found Jesus in my heart,' he answered.

We parted at the railways crossing and as we said our goodbyes I decided not to reinforce that it was never my intention to jump. It felt better to let him keep my soul as one that he had saved. It was my gift to him for trying.

*

I WALKED BACK TO WHERE I had abandoned my car in the alley. A note had been left pushed under the wipers. It was crudely written; obviously from a resident whose way I had blocked; whose rules I had broken.

Soon, I was pulling into the courtyard of the hotel car park. My room was all paid-up until tomorrow so there was nothing strange with me returning.

The maid hurried across the courtyard. She noticed me and gave a huge smile before disappearing through a doorway to the spiral staircase.

I went to the attic room. I felt exhausted by my exertion; my upper legs ached and my shoes felt like they were full of marbles. I smelt too. Yet my mind was surprisingly clear, almost to the point of being vacant. It was as if it had gone on over-load and like a computer had been re-set. I lay on the bed and slept only to be awoken some hours later by the sound of music coming through the open window from the bar below.

'Let me buy you a drink,' I said to Herr Ovel as I perched on a stool at the bar. He turned from another customer and stretched his short arm across the counter to shake my hand. I was relieved he did not know or had chosen not to mention that I had involved his wife in my deception; perhaps she had not told him.

'You are leaving tomorrow?' I wondered whether it was a request.

'Maybe not,' I said, looking straight at him. I was eager to check his response. Yet he just smiled again and turned to serve other customers.

As the evening progressed the bar began to fill. A couple walked in shaking the creases from their coats before hanging them up on the coat stand by the door. They bid the bar Güten arbend and waved to Herr Ovel before taking a table.

Some minutes later two workmen were brushing their feet on the mat. Both were wearing tight, low cut, double-buttoned waistcoats, traditional to German tradesmen. They gave me a nod of recognition.

Everyone seemed friendly that night, everyone who entered bid everybody 'Guten arbend'. Perhaps it was the calm after such a traumatic day or the immediate feeling of relief that comes from finally knowing one's fate and limitations; more likely my feeling of warmth towards the German people came from the complimentary schnapps that Herr Ovel offered in-between every glass of tall frothy beer.

These were nice Germans, I thought, not the bad ones I had seen that morning in the courtroom. After my speech to the judge, after I had heroically ended my statement with *They are not your children,* the looks of boiling contempt had been overwhelming.

Eva, predictably, shot daggers across the room and Frau Meier grimaced with disdain while theatrically shaking her head slowly from side to side; an impressive reaction intended more for the judge. The assistant frantically whispered into the judge's ear while both were staring at me.

Otto, on the other hand did not seem flustered by my speech. His eyes had widened as if watching a car crash yet he retained an expression that I took to be expectancy; it was not how he reacted but how he didn't; never once trying to stare me down as he had in the past or beckon me into silence with an under table tap on my shoe.

'You spoke with your heart,' he said squeezing a hand on my shoulder. 'So now the decision is out of your hands and indeed out of your ex-wife's too. Because you have refused to sign an agreement then the judge must decide what is in the...'

'...best interests of the children.' I finished the sentence for him.

Judge Heinrich left the court and everybody stood up except me. Otto pulled me to my feet as she passed.

'What happens now?' I loudly whispered in frustration.

'I will explain everything to you in private,' Otto said, eyeing Frau Meier who, like Eva, was gathering papers and preparing to leave.

'Do I get to see my children,' I said loudly. Eva and Frau Meier stared at me with blank faces. Otto answered in a lower tone.

'Yes, I am sure the judge will allow you to see your children but the arrangements for this will be given in due cause.'

'Another wait,' I snarled, like a dog.

I WAS SOON OUTSIDE BREATHING the cold damp air. I had beaten the elevators by running down the stairs and pushed so hard on the revolving doors that a lady entering had to go around again. I needed to get out, not only from the building but also the country.

I wanted to head home with my children; the autobahn stretched out before me, England on the horizon growing steadily closer.

*

HERR OVEL OFFERED ANOTHER SCHNAPPS. The sickly sweet aniseed tingled my lips as I swallowed it in one before slamming the shot glass back down on the bar like a Russian. With every drink I became hazy and unsteady on the stool, then she was sitting next to me although I didn't recall her coming in. Her brown eyes seemed larger than normal and I fell into them. We joked a lot or rather I joked and she politely giggled whether she understood the humour or not. We sat close, so close in fact that our knees were touching. She asked about my children and I became solemn. Her sincere expression was moving and I was thankful that she reverted back to laughter when I purposely changed the subject.

'You are a good man,' she said playfully poking me on the chest.

I became far drunker than her, if indeed she was drunk at all. I jumped off my stool and swayed and she was quick to help. Her small size fit snug under my arm when helping me up the spiral staircase to my bedroom. I was too uncoordinated to navigate the key into the lock and she took charge of that too. Once in the room I heard the door slam behind me and turned to see that she had followed me in. We stood in silence. I slid my arms around her waist as her arms in turn wrapped around my neck. The moon that shone through the skylight glistened on her glassy brown eyes. I could feel her heart beating onto mine.

'You are the first woman I have held since Eva,' I said quietly.

'Eva, this is the name of your wife?' I did not answer.

'I have a boyfriend too,' she said, 'but not in this country.' Then we kissed and I could taste the liquorice shots we had been drinking.

In the distance I heard slam of the door at the bottom of the spiral staircase followed by the rapid slap of leather soles on marble. The light from under the door lit up the room. There was a sudden knock.

'Herr Archer, Herr Archer,' came the familiar voice of Herr Ovel. 'There is a telephone call for you from England. It's from a man called Dave, he says it's bloody urgent.'

Chapter 21

A SHARP FROST HAD TAKEN the country by surprise. Lasting for two days, it had hardened the ground to such a degree that it made grave digging impossible, even for a mechanical digger. Normally, in late November, Dave assured me, the biggest problem in excavating a site was to avoid churning up the ground around the hole and making it dangerous for mourners to slip in.

'Maybe I should be a grave digger,' stated Dave as we waited by the black wrought iron gate at the entrance to cemetery. Michael soon arrived with other faces I recognized from the car park protest. We were all dressed solemnly in black suits, which, if not outside a graveyard would make us look like gangsters.

'Good of you to make it,' Michael said while shaking my hand. I felt irritated that he had acted as if it was upon his request that I had attended.

'It's a sad day for us all,' he continued, 'that one of our own should take his life.'

We walked in silence through the cemetery towards the chapel; the only sound was the soft crunch of gravel. The outer part of the graveyard was old and unkempt with tombstones leaning left and right, backwards and forwards in the sunken ground. Gradually, as we neared the chapel, the graves became upright and the head stones smoother. The cold bit into the ends of my fingers.

Michael, leading the group, stopped and directed us all to stand along the road. A hearse approached followed by four other cars and all quietly glided passed. A woman in the back of the lead car buried her head in a tissue. Dave began to raise his hand to salute. I grabbed his arm.

'It's not a military funeral,' I growled.

We all decided to wait a respectful distance from the chapel entrance to allow the family to gather. The coffin was unloaded and then skilfully lifted onto the shoulders of four men. John explained in whispers to us all that at the request of his wife, we should not attend the service.

'She thinks it's our fault,' he said. 'She said that we put,' he emphasized the next two words, *'unrealistic expectations* into his head and made him feel desperate.'

The word *desperate* rang in my ears as only days previously, I had heard Otto say it to me. The two daughters, both under the age of ten, wore fluffy white dresses with matching bows. They held a bouquet of flowers and walked in step as they followed the coffin of their father.

'What a messed-up world,' I said 'when a daddy feels so distraught without his own children that he would rather not live, than live without them.' No-one answered. Everyone just stared at the black suits and long dark dresses that filed into the chapel.

We remained standing in reverent silence until the last mourner had walked in. Michael spoke with a bitterness I had not heard before.

'I know what the headlines will say,' he said. 'Disturbed father; mentally ill, unstable. They will probably blame it on drink and hint towards violence and the children will grow up hating the memory of their Dad.'

We all listened but said nothing; each one of us in our own thoughts. I pondered on the gritty reality of my new world. Some fathers, I thought, do not have the strength to rebuild their lives without their children. Some cannot switch from seeing their children every day to every second weekend; spending endless hours, days and weeks without them; slowly losing touch. Young people can grow half an inch and lose a tooth between visits, speak more words; know more things, things that we have no influence over. And where will they live and whom will they live with, I thought? Which religion? Which school will they go to, what languages will they speak or in which country they reside? All of this daily life is gone; all these decisions can be taken away till you are barely a parent at all.

If the father runs, he is a bastard for abandoning his children. If he stays he must submit and pay; play a parental part that is determined by the mother and the court. A weekend father, a Disney Dad. *Buy me another milkshake or take me home;* a shadow of a father.

Yet for some, for Henry, the only decision left was not to choose that life at all.

I turned to look at the men around me, all of whom had mist in their eyes, all thinking of their own children and perhaps, in their bleakest thoughts, remembering a time, like myself, when I felt as desperate as Henry did.

'How did it happen? I asked. Michael told us of Henry's sad demise and as we listened, the sound of a hymn gently seeped from the chapel windows.

'It was a van driver that found Henry's body in his car, slumped over the steering wheel, in, of all places, McDonald's car park. Henry had taken the girls there but one of them felt tired so he had to take them back to their mother early. Later that evening Henry returned and parked his car in the dark corner where the overhead light was broken. He then attached a pipe to the end of the exhaust and poked it through the passenger window. Nobody noticed. His body wasn't discovered till the following morning.'

'Now that's desperate,' said Dave, his breath steaming in the cold morning air.

I spoke without thinking, 'I know the feeling.' Dave suddenly looked at me. I quickly shook my head. 'Don't worry,' I assured him 'I'd never do that.'

A smile grew over his face. 'You could never do it in my van anyway, the exhaust has blown.' Forgetting where we were, we both shared a gallow's laugh until a scornful glare from Michael shot us into silence.

A man came running over.

'It's a bit emotional in there,' he said, jerking a thumb towards the chapel. 'The girls are screaming for their Daddy. So leave it for today, boys. You can come and pay your respects at the grave site another time.'

It was decided between us that we should give Henry a good send-off down the pub. He would have liked that, somebody said. So we slowly dispersed from the cemetery in groups of twos and threes. I declined a lift in Michael's car and instead peeled away with Dave and began to walk. I needed to move my body, still stiff after my long journey back from Germany.

It had taken almost two days from leaving the Hotel in Ahrensburg before I was finally rumbling over the metal gang plank at Harwich docks. I had boarded the huge vessel the previous afternoon at the port of Hamburg. As the massive liner pushed off, I sat on the top deck and watched Germany drifting away as if it was the ship, and we were standing still.

I could have easily stowed my children onto this vessel, I thought, and the rabbit too. The passport check seemed more of a formality than a necessity. A young customs officer, wearing a green cap, barely leaned out of the wooden box at the entrance to the harbour. He casually scanned my passport. He did not even look into the back seat of the car where I had purposely piled up blankets and clothes to test the security.

I parked my car in the belly of the ship and walked up the narrow stairs to the upper decks. It was comforting to hear English spoken again, a sensation akin to someone hard of hearing being fitted with a hearing aid, although there seemed to be a lot of German males on the boat too.

One young English family, seated by the life boats, were clearly ready to go home. Both husband and wife were holding a small child, which they used like a ventriloquist's dummy when arguing.

'When we get home,' the mother said, 'we can go and see grandma and tell her how your daddy flirted with the waitress.'

'Yes, grandma will be happy to take Mummy's side,' said the father looking into the child's eyes, 'grandma doesn't like daddy and daddy doesn't like her...' And so it continued.

My cabin for the night was on the inner deck with no porthole. There was nothing to distract my thoughts away from Henry. Had he really killed himself? I thought. It seemed unbelievable at the time.

The cabin walls vibrated and began to sway slightly. I noticed the sick-bags that were placed under the pillows on the bunks so decided to stretch my legs in one of the corridors on the upper decks where I could smell the sea.

'I could never be a sailor,' I confessed to Dave as we turned into the high street. He had listened intently to my story about my journey back from Germany.

'I get sick on the Isle of Wight ferry,' Dave said, then added thoughtfully, 'You should have just taken your kids and left the rabbit.'

We reached the designated pub and just before Dave went to push open the glass door I stopped and turned to him.

'It wasn't just the rabbit. My children are becoming foreign to me. They will soon be more German than English. I'm losing them, Dave.'

He held open the door and allowed me to walk in first. I had expecting to see a crowd of suited men standing in the corner in reverent silence, solemnly sipping dark warm beer. Yet instead I was greeted with a cheer of enthusiasm. The pub was full, mainly of men, most in working clothes. Wooden chairs had been placed in rows. One of the lads from the father's group, who I didn't recall seeing at the funeral, waved us over to some seats.

'You are just in time for the match,' he said. I could see Michael over at the bar, deep in conversation. Dave dipped a hand into his pocket and jangled something into my hand.

'Look after my keys mate,' he said. 'I think it's going to get messy and I always lose my house keys when I get drunk.' We walked to some seats.

'You took your time,' said Michael as he shouldered passed me with a tray full of beers.

'Hurry up and sit down before the national anthems start,' somebody shouted from the back.

A growing amount of men began to settle in front of a large TV on the wall. From behind the bar the landlord pointed his remote control. A sudden vision of a huge football stadium filled the screen. The cameras scanned along a line of nervously waiting football players, some chewing gum, other jumping on the spot.

There were some scruffy young lads seated close to the front. One was wearing a dirty high viz t-shirt and had obviously come straight from work. He half turned back to the pub and said, 'There is no such thing as a friendly match when we're playing Germany.'

A huge German flag was passed across the heads of the fans on one side of the stadium. The TV commenter said something about the masses of Germans that had travelled over to England. I recalled the large amount of young Germans on the ferry crossing.

Some of the men in the pub rose to their feet, holding their hands to their hearts and their beer bellies in, as *God save the Queen* blared out from the television. Then came the national German anthem and everybody whistled. I turned to Dave.

'We are supposed to be here to honour Henry.' Dave shrugged his shoulders.

'We are, Henry would have loved this.' Perhaps he was right, I thought, although I did not recall Henry following football.

The English football team, as far as I could make out, were out-played by the German team right from the first blow of the whistle. People around the pub gnawed their nails and slapped their thighs at every missed pass.

The German strikers positively peppered the English goal line, yet the defence held, giving encouragement to the excited fans around the pub. At the other end of the pitch the German goalkeeper had to perform star jumps to keep warm. There is a forlorn hope, I thought, that exists only when watching football and especially when it's England playing.

Come half-time the score remained nil, nil and a feeling of cautious optimism spread around the pub; people who had been transfixed on the screen rested their eyes. This optimism was soon to be crushed. In the second half the German team played with extra flow and agility. Before any of us could settle into our seats, with a missed tackle by an English defender and a floating pass from one German striker to another, the ball whacked into the goal, caught like a salmon. It was met around the pub with groans and shaking heads. Many of the calls of encouragement now turned to abuse, not only to the English players but also the Germans. A few of the drunker men at the front began to sing:

Two world wars and one world cup.

Two world wars and one world cup.
What's it like to win a war.

As the game continued the German players grew more confident and scored again. The stadium on the German side erupted and the camera panned in on numerous elated German fans, their enlarged faces filling the screen. The abuse from the pub was now directed not at the players but at their country.

I felt ashamed and thought of Otto waiting for me in the bar, Frau Ovel baking a cake and the taxi driver with his fat hand patting my head. If they were here now, I thought, I'd sink into the wall.

The men at the very front continued to shout *bloody Germans, sauerkraut scum.* I looked at Dave seated behind me for comfort. He, at first, smirked through his bushy beard then read my anguish.

'You okay mate,' he whispered into my ear, barely audible over the sound of the chanting.

'My children are German,' I answered pitifully.

The men at the front stood up, all with t-shirts rising above their lower bellies. One of then glugged down his pint and started shouting 'Bloody Nazis.' I hid my face in dismay.

Dave put a hand on my shoulder and stood up. He spoke in a loud unfamiliar voice, his accent taken from one of the many black and white war films.

'Come on zee Germans,' he shouted. Immediately the three men at the front turned around.

'Jawohl, I am zee German and I have zee German children. You want to make problem with me?' Dave rolled his fists in front of him. Then another member of our group stood up and announced, 'I am zee German too.' Then another. It was a scene taken from the film Spartacus. Soon all of the men from our group stood up around me proclaimed to be German.

Dave, in his undersize suit and bushy beard cut an awesome figure. He was a bear of a man who had once balanced three bags of cement on his head. The scruffiest and loudest man amongst the three at the front puffed out his chest and began to chant again. '*Two world wars and one world cup. Two world wars and one world cup.*'

I urged Dave to sit down, not to bother; the idiot was just drunk, I explained. Yet everyone remained standing. Dave, not knowing the words, began to hum the German national anthem. The others soon joined in. Most were wearing their black funeral suits so may have looked like a choir. I was moved almost to tears. If my children could see me now, I thought. Then the Germans scored again and everybody stopped singing.

THE FINAL WHISTLE BLEW AND the pub emptied like a cinema. Everyone from the funeral gathered at the bar. Michael raised his glass.

'To Henry!' he said, and we held our glasses aloft and remembered the solemn reason for our suits.

Michael spoke of action, of another protest; a bigger demonstration to catch the eye of the press: to hold up traffic, blockade a bridge. 'We will dedicate it to Henry,' he said, 'and wear printed t-shirts with his name on.'

I didn't believe that we would do anything for Henry but I was drunk and pretending to do something felt better than to do nothing at all. We toasted Henry again and later again until we were all satisfied that something had been done.

The few that remained as the night continued staggered in a circle around a table. A crowd of ladies walked in screaming with laughter. They strutted in a line. A few gave curious smiles at our suited appearance then settled around a table at the far end of the bar where soon two bottles, set in ice were placed on their table.

'How many of those women have taken children away from their fathers?' said Michael. Everybody looked scornfully over. One of the women was filling the fluted glasses. She said something and they all roared with laughter.

I looked down at the tabled and cursed the reality of my new world. Fortunately, it would only be hours before I would learn that a separated mother has woes of her own.

Chapter 22

THE QUEUE WAS PURPOSELY POSITIONED on the darkened unlit side of the street where only the glow of a cigarette showed the ghostly contours of a man's face.

'I'm not going in,' I said. 'It's not my cup of tea.'

There were a few jeers from some younger lads further down in the line. Dave, in his drunken state tried to encourage me to stay but I staggered off in search of the taxi. Within two streets I found a line of hazy brake lights. Each taxi, in turn, pulled to the front of the queue and was promptly, although not elegantly, filled with its drunken cargo. A couple in front of me argued with the taxi driver to be allowed on-board with their kebabs. I waited patiently and dug my hands in my trouser pockets and found an unfamiliar bunch of keys. I cursed aloud.

Within a few minutes I was back outside the darkened doorway trying to persuade a huge bouncer to let me in. He looked right through me.

'Can't you just make an announcement and ask for Dave to come to the door to collect his keys?' I asked.

'You must be joking,' said the bouncer with a deep guttural laugh. 'Most people in here wouldn't admit to being in here.'

A tiny girl wearing a skirt so short that it may have been a t-shirt was perched on a stool behind reinforced glass. She took my money without looking into my eyes then a huge dark man pulled back a curtain and waved me through.

A flash from a glitter ball that hung from the ceiling dazzled me. The place was dark and smelled of unvented rooms. In the distance there was a raised platform with electric blue neon strips stuck to surrounding mirrored walls. I could hear the background thump of stereo music, dry ice and men's tobacco coughs.

In the dim light I vaguely recognized the postman who delivered down my road. I had normally thought of him as a meek and humble man, known for talking endlessly about his exotic fish. I had never seen him without his official uniform that always had the top button tightly done up.

Yet, here, the postman, in this dark and seedy world built under the railway viaduct, was a different person. He languished under the stage with his sunglasses perched on his head and his shirt unbuttoned half way down. He had a roll of bank notes sticking out from his top pocket and would often toss some cash onto the tray of the waitress if they smiled when serving his drink, and they always smiled.

All the while the glistening, twinkling tiny stars imprinted on the bikini bottoms reflected off the surrounding mirrors as the young topless female turned on a pole like a spinning top. I noticed Michael with a few others over by the bar and joined them.

'I knew you would come,' said Michael. His comments instantly annoyed me.

'Can you give Dave his keys?' I said holding them out. There was a loud clap from a single person that took the attention of us all. The postman was applauding the end of a performance. I turned to our crowd and said, 'He's a postman, not a mafia boss.'

'He's always in here,' Michael said.

'You been here before?'

Michael's cheeks flushed. 'Only a couple of times after Caroline left, just to keep my hand in.'

'Hand in what?' I asked.

Michael ignored my question. 'The beer's good too,' he said.

I stood nestled in the middle of the crowd of men like an embarrassed schoolboy. There were other huddles of men around the bar, each with a couple of pretty girls dressed in leotards who buzzed like bees or rather hunted like hyenas around the packs, trying to catch the eye of the weaker men and distract them away from the herd for a private dance.

I want to go home, I thought. I want to go back to my wife and children. Walk into the kitchen in the morning and see them around the table; for it all to be normal again. Not be in this seedy and smelly world with a carpet spongy with beer.

I pushed my way out, momentarily dazzled by a flash from the glitter ball. I clipped the silver tray of a passing waitress. It bounced on the carpet making the sound of a gong. I fell to my knees and quickly began to help gather the plastic glasses.

'I'll do it,' came a familiar voice. I looked up.

'My god, Helen, what are you doing here?'

*

SOME HOURS LATER I WAS waiting by the back entrance of the establishment. A single light above the door shone a semi-circle on the ground. I was not the only man waiting in the shadows; two others were shifting uneasily from side to side. Occasionally we glanced at the others, like gun fighters in a spaghetti western. One of them held a bunch of garage forecourt flowers in his hand.

There was a clunk of an unoiled door handle and we all looked up. A girl stepped into the light, blowing cigarette smoke from her nose, which dispersed around her blonde frizzy hair making it look as though her head was steaming. The man with the flowers moved forward.

'Oh sweetie, you shouldn't have,' she said in an overtly childish voice. She drew heavily on her cigarette before linking arms with him and they walked off into the darkness of the nearby car park.

I waited for some moments afterwards and was about to lose my nerve and leave when Helen appeared. She was dressed in a full-length coat with the collar turn up. I stepped forward and smiled but it wasn't returned.

'You nearly got me fired, running out like that,' she said sharply. 'Do you know how difficult it is for me to get a job? Lucky for me, the glasses were empty.'

'You like working at that place?' It was a provocative answer and I regretted it. Helen stared daggers into me and began to walk.

'I see it wasn't beneath you to go in,' she said.

I quickly begged her forgiveness and followed her down the road like a scorned puppy. She looked beautiful although tired and the make-up, which lay thick around the eyes, did little to conceal this. I walked with her to the car park and she stopped beside a small yellow mini with a dent in the wing. I noticed a child seat in the back. I casually offered that we might find a place for coffee. This bought a smile to her face and she rolled her eyes comically.

'I think you've seen enough women for one night,' she said.

'But I didn't,' I answered, 'I wouldn't. I'm not like the others. They are just a bunch of hypocrites, well maybe not Dave, but the rest are. The whole place is full of...' While I was ranting Helen had climbed into her car and started the engine. The electric window slowly moved down.

'I've got a daughter,' she said, 'a little girl, and this is the only way I can pay for her. She sleeps at my mother's while I work here. The money is good, Richard, and I don't have to beg her father for it.' There was venom in her last sentence and she looked to see my reaction. I was bound to ask.

187

'Do you let the father see your daughter?' Helen breathed out heavily.

'I heard about your situation, I feel very sorry for you but not all fathers are like you, Richard. Some couldn't care less. Some don't even bother seeing their child or paying any support for them, yet they are in there throwing money at the girls.'

She paused for a moment and looked at me with pity in her eyes. I had seen this expression so many times, of late, in people when talking to me; their heads leaning to one side, their tone an octave lower.

'I hope you get your children back from Germany,' she said. I swallowed hard. She shifted into first and gave a forlorn smile. Then she drove out of the car park; our last view of each other was through the rear view mirror.

Chapter 23

CHRISTMAS WAS FAST APPROACHING AND in the preceding weeks every seasonal nuance and ritual increased on a daily basis: from tinsel in the shop windows to festive songs on the radio. *It's the most wonderful time of year* played in the supermarket as I shopped for food. Although for me Christmas was cancelled, and I ignored it at every turn.

Yet it was impossible to avoid the subject when speaking with Louise and Sebastian on the phone. They had yet to grasp the fact that any Christmas with daddy would be conducted in a hotel bedroom, if the courts allowed me access at all.

I still had no correspondence from Otto concerning the judge's decision. Every morning I sifted through the mail that dropped upon my doormat like a pack of cards.

I had continued to speak to them twice weekly, always making sure that I phoned during shop opening times to ensure the receiver would be picked up. It was extremely expensive, with extortionate overseas telephone rates I could ill afford; therefore my conversations with them were sometimes painfully short. Often they would swap to German half-way through a sentence, especially Sebastian. Most of the time I led the conversation, telling them about my day, trying to invent interesting stories to retain their attention. I was becoming a play father, the funny man that phoned twice a week and who kept them occupied until a sharp German voice in the background would call them away. Eva never came to the phone. Her mother would always pick up the receiver from the shop.

'Can I speak to my children please.' I always made a point of saying *my children*. There was never any recognition that I was on the line, just a sharp bark in German, which I presume was Omar shouting up the stairs for one of the children to pick up.

This was the sum total of my family life for December, leading up to Christmas. I was lost in a void, an empty no-mans-land wandering from one telephone conversation to the other; arriving home from work to sit on the bottom step of the stairs to speak to my children; my veins transfused with their voices.

Sometimes little snippets of information gleaned from one of them would be brandished the following day at tea break. Other fathers often spoke about their kids: bedtime tantrums, their cute-as-buttons comments at the dinner table. Sebastian had told me that he had met a new friend at kindergarten called Ansam; it was a passing comment that he never repeated; yet at work I used it to be normal.

'My son is settling in well at school,' I would say, 'he has a new friend called Ansam. Lovely lad.' And for a moment I was like all the other dads.

I continued in this empty way, not knowing how to stop, not knowing how to go forward. I was running on empty, a shadow of myself.

Then Christmas was only days away and I was preparing to lock myself in until it was over; metaphorically board up the windows and nail a sign on my front door: *Plague*. I was losing my children drip by drip.

Quite unexpectedly I arrived home late one evening after work to see the flashing light on my answering machine. Otto's voice was quick and excited.

'I told you to trust me,' he said. 'I told you I had a brick in her wall. We are of the same tribe, her and me. Call me as soon as…' A sharp beeeep abruptly ended the message.

I frantically tapped the phone number of his office in the vain hope that he might be working late but alas heard the recorded greeting from his secretary. Then I remembered that he had given me his home number on the day of the picnic when he was natural. A brief vision of Otto walking naked through the forest flashed through my head. I tore upstairs and rummaged through the pockets of my backpack in search for the number, and in the bottom of the bag found a crumpled piece of serviette that Otto had written upon.

It was his wife who answered. Strange that I could never imagine Otto having one, although he often spoke affectionately about her. She impressively swapped to English on hearing my voice and asked me to wait while she fetched Otto. She used my first name although I had not offered it so Otto had obviously been talking about me.

I paced back and forth, nervously leashed to the machine by a curly wire. Eventually I heard Otto clear his throat, a habit I had witnessed in the courtroom.

'My dear friend,' he said, 'it is a good day because it is me that you have.'

He began to explain, in his own way, the situation that now presented itself. As usual with Otto, he would go off on a tangent and speak of his time with the Sioux Indians, how he wept in the forest and prayed to the same moon that his children could see in Germany. I was desperate for information and forever coaxing him back on the subject.

'So the judge is on my side?' I asked feeling incredulous even to be questioning it.

'She is on no-one's side,' Otto confirmed. 'But she was impressed with you, I knew she would be. That is why I got *you* to make a stand.' Otto allowed the statement to sink in.

'You knew I would refuse to sign the agreement?'

'I know the English; Lord Nelson, Churchill. You would rather fight and lose, than surrender.' Otto began to explain that after I had walked out of the consultation room he allowed Frau Meier to believe that he was desperate to get me to sign anything. 'So naturally Frau Meier, being greedy, drew up a contract with outrageous demands benefitting only her own client and Eva was happy to go along with it. I even persuaded her to include the words *German children,* pretending that it was to help you accept the fact that your children were living there. Yet I knew this, in reality would get up your back and make you refuse.' Otto then corrected himself. 'That is to say, I had every hope you would refuse and therefore be bound by the judge's decision, who can only intervene when two parties cannot agree. Which is what we wanted all along. I told you I have a brick in her wall.'

As Otto continued to talk I sat down on the bottom of the stairs. My knees had actually become weak and wobbled, a sensation up until then I believed only existed in cartoons. My emotions were at the top of my throat. I begged Otto to repeat his last sentence.

'Yes, my friend, you can take your children home for Christmas. Richard ..... Richard...... are you there?'

I finally croaked a response and Otto continued. He spoke in a softer tone and explained that the judge had understood my lack of payment towards the children.

'I told her of your expensive plane flights and hotel fees,' Otto said. Then his tone became sterner. 'But starting January you must pay every month.' I eagerly agreed and began to shower thanks upon him yet Otto continued in his serious fashion.

'Be warned my English friend. If, for whatever reason, you do not take your children home for Christmas, it will be difficult for me to persuade the court to give you another chance. The judge is allowing you to set your own precedent. She is giving you a chance to be the father you say you are. But your wife's counsel will know this too. I am not saying they will try and put a stop to it but it would be to their benefit if you do not leave the country with your children, if you do not set that precedent. Then you will be back to one square.'

'Square one,' I corrected. I paused. 'Can Eva legally stop me? Can Frau Meier appeal?'

'Perhaps,' Otto answered, 'but not until after Christmas. I have known about this decision for weeks and managed to persuade the judge to delay telling your wife's counsel until now. I told you I have a brick in her wall. If there is to be an appeal then it will have to wait until after Christmas because the courts are now shut for the holidays, so they cannot stop you until after Christmas by which time your precedent will be set.'

I was taken aback by his ingenuity. This apparently silly man, who walked naked in the forest and spoke of the Sioux Indians, was in reality stealthy and shrewd. I couldn't help but wonder if it was all an act.

Otto raised his voice and announcing in a jovial tone, 'Come to Germany my friend and collect your children, Otto Lehmann has won the day for England.'

I had a feeling that his theatrics may have been for his wife's ears, who, no doubt, would be listening to test her own English.

I began to thank him, pour compliments down the phone yet Otto was quick to explain the rules. 'This is Germany,' he said, 'for sure, there are rules.'

I was to pick the children up on the morning of the twenty-fifth and not before. It was fortunate in this case, the judge had explained to Otto in her Solomon-like wisdom, that Germany celebrates their Christmas on the 24th and England on the 25th. Therefore we could share. Otto finished his conversation with a stark sombre warning.

'And remember Richard, after your Christmas holiday, bring them back.'

Chapter 24

LATE THE FOLLOWING MORNING OF the 22nd, I arrived outside the airport terminal in Dave's rusty van. He purposely parked at the far end of the main entrance to avoid his vehicle being recognized for his previous illegal parking.

'I can't thank you enough,' I said, jumping out of the van. 'I will repay you the money for the flights.' Dave shrugged his shoulder. I believe he was holding his emotions back.

'Go and get your children mate,' he said with a croak. Then as he drove off he shouted out the window, 'I'd have only spent the money on strippers.'

I waved him off as a gust of winter wind starkly freshened my face as if water had been splashed against it.

With a whoosh, the glass doors parted and I stepped into the mass of moving people and was sucked along as if carried by a strong tide. The busy terminal was in stark contrast to the sleepy villages we had just driven though. Everybody seemed to be heading in one direction, then suddenly another. Some people, oblivious to the flow, stood like rocks in the rapids reading their printed itineraries while everyone else bashed around them. Father Christmas hats were everywhere and others had tinsel draped onto their shoulders or around their bags; in the distance a busy coffee outlet played Christmas carols to blurry-eyed customers.

There was a printed map on a wall of the airport lay-out and I searched with my finger for Air Berlin: the only airline that still had suitable flights.

After hearing Otto on the answering machine, I had spent the following morning franticly phoning airlines. I had paid heavily for three seats on the very last flight out of Hamburg on Christmas Day, one of only two flights leaving that day.

Yet with my outbound flight to Hamburg I had no such options; I either flew today or not at all on this side of the holidays. It seemed that everyone wanted to go home for Christmas.

After the check-in desk and the endless security queues I was finally buckling my seat belt and praying that the plane had sufficient thrust to lift its fully packed human cargo into the air.

I slept uneasily on the flight. A German fellow with a pencil moustache sitting next to me tried endlessly to entice me into conversation, no doubt for his last opportunity to practice his English. I wondered whether the hairs above his lip were stunted or had been purposely shaven back.

'I have an English girlfriend,' he stated. I smiled to myself as I feigned sleep and considered that if he were to marry his English girlfriend, his life might turn out like mine, only in reverse.

The plane landed with a violent bump and I noted that the passengers must have been overwhelmingly Germany as nobody made a joke about it. This time I arrived at Hamburg International, which was far more bustling than Lübeck airport. I followed the crowds to passport control and practiced my usual blank expression to the customs officer before waiting for my bag to appear through the plastic curtains like a game show.

The exit led into the airport's large airy foyer, which was the size of a skating rink. At one end stood an enormous Christmas tree some ten metres high; at the other end, through the glass door could be seen the busy streets of Hamburg. As I walked I looked up at the ceilings. The criss-cross girders seemed so high that a kicked football would not reach it. I found a row of three public phones hanging from the wall and tapped out a number from a card.

Once outside I felt the sharp decrease in temperature press upon my face. After twenty minutes of waiting my nose began to sting. The cold was a stark reminder of the approaching snow that my fellow passenger on the plane had predicted.

A few taxis came and went until I saw the familiar face. He pulled up alongside and waved a meaty hand in recognition. I was determined to use him for my taxi after the kindness he had shown me. He gestured for me to sit in the front seat.

'You come see die kinder?' he asked.

'I've come to take them home,' I answered proudly.

'Wunderbar,' he stated while pulling into the traffic. The single windscreen wiper of his Mercedes swiped the sleet with incredible speed. The taxi driver looked up to the sky with a tut tut. The daylight was rapidly fading. Within ten minutes of city driving, the Christmas decorations that were strewn across shop doorways or suspended on wires high above the road began to glow. We passed the main harbour that was vast and still, covered in a blanket of forming ice. A little tugboat pushed through the flat black water cutting a line in its wake.

Approaching Ahrensburg from the south was a twenty minute drive from Hamburg, in a route that never broke into countryside. The Bahnhof station, not the castle, was the first landmark I recognised.

The taxi pulled behind a small line of cars as we waited out the familiar ting ting ting at the white railway crossing gate. Eventually the gated lifted, its red lights flashing. The taxi rumbled over the tracks before slowing to a stop by the cobbled pavement.

'You walking from here, alles clar?' he asked. The taxi driver again looked up to the falling sleet, eager to get away.

'No problem,' I said, handing him the fare. I asked about my return journey.

'Arbeiten jede tag,' he said before swapping to English. 'Working every day.'

I made arrangements with him in accordance to the strict instructions Otto had laid down for me: He was to appear with his yellow taxi outside of the shop at 10am of the 25th, not a moment before. I explained this to the taxi driver as if I was a schoolteacher. He listened intently and nodded. One of the beauties, I thought, of being in Germany is that people do not take offence when given exact instructions.

As the taxi drove away I noticed that the tyres were already cutting tracks in the gathering snow. I turned my collar up and began to scurry the short distance to Hotel No6. I had the immediate worry that I might accidently bump into my children, who, by cruel coincidence might just happen to be passing.

I recalled Otto's instructions: the rules of engagement. There was to be no contact what-so-ever with the children during the 'mother's time' of the Christmas holiday. If I were, in anyway, to bend or break this rule it may give reason for the children not to be handed over on the 25th.

'Stick to the rules,' Otto had warned, then added, 'And no hiding in the bushes.' I had offered no answer to Otto, as I had never admitted that it was me in the garden. I trudged down the alley.

There were no usual welcoming lights shining from the bar at the end of the courtyard. Everything was uncommonly quiet and still. Also, apart from my own dragging footprints there were no others to spoil the virgin fluttering of sleet. I rattled the door to the bar, my hand sticking to the cold doorknob and pressed my face against the window. It was dark inside and unused, spotlessly clean with chairs unturned on the tables. I walked across the courtyard to the door leading to the spiral staircase, and it too was locked.

My accommodation was the one thing I had not arranged, it was the one thing I thought I did not need to… Hotels don't usually close for Christmas, I had supposed.

I pulled the tattered brown envelope that Dave had given me from my pocket, and counted his hard-earned money. There was sixty pound in English money, which normally would have been sufficient to pay for two nights in the attic room, with breakfast. Herr Ovel was always happy to exchange British sterling.

I undid zips and checked pockets, my movements slow and clumsy as the cold began to affect my fingers. I found only a few Deutsch Marks, most of which I would have to save for the taxi back to the airport. As I blew on my hands snowflakes settled on my shoulders. At the end of the alleyway in the street I could see families walking past with colourful coats and bobble hats. I envied that they had somewhere to go.

My leather shoes were not designed for the snow and the damp began to soak into my socks as I walked across town. By the time I arrived on the plush carpet of Hotel Am Schloss my feet were blocks of ice. I took a moment to stand by a heater to warm my body before the blue eyes of the high cheek-boned receptionist prompted me into conversation.

I asked for a room but she quickly assured me that my budget would only pay for a single room for one night.

'Perhaps try Hamburg,' she stated before turned her attention to an elderly couple in fur-lined coats who had just entered through the sliding doors, brushing snow from their shoulders. I reluctantly stepped back out into the cold breeze.

It was now completely dark and although the snow had stopped falling, its effects muffled Ahrensburg city life with only the odd car slowly crunching by, and a lone person wrapped in warm clothing heading to a warm house.

I thought of my children. They loved snow and would have their noses pressed to their bedroom windows watching it fall. A thought occurred to me: I had never yet had a snowball fight with them or taken them sledging. Yet my cold feet dominated my thoughts, so I dipped my head in the direction of the Bahnhof Station Cafeteria and stopped only at the white gates of the railway crossing. The cold rush from a passing train blasted my face. As I approached the cafeteria I could see the silhouettes of the inhabitants through the steamed up windows, their stretched shadows dancing in the snow.

A few people looked up from their soups as I entered, blue with cold. The smell was intoxicating, a mixture of strong coffee, Weiss beer and lightly fried sausage meat. I had not eaten since that morning and my mouth salivated. The counter that hugged one side of the café had people sitting along it, drinking and eating, dipping bread into bowls. I asked the bartender for a coffee. It was all I could afford yet the half-empty plate that he cleared away I would have gladly licked clean.

I wrapped my hands around the mug of coffee, causing shooting chilblains. The feeling of despair was overwhelming and I felt thankful there was no-one to pity me; I felt sure I would have succumbed to tears.

I re-counted the money in the brown envelope, scattering its contents on the counter. I only had enough for one night in the expensive hotel, yet if I were to do that, then I would be homeless on Christmas eve; quite literally, mimicking the seasonal biblical story: 'There's no place at the inn.'

I finished my coffee and left. The smell of food was killing me and I could not trust myself not to finish the soup of the man sitting next to me when he went to the toilet.

The snow had not started again with only odd flurries whipped off the rooftops by the gathering breeze. I would spend one night in the expensive hotel, I thought, and then the next day I would eat a feast at breakfast that would last all day.

I wanted to walk by the shop on the way back to the hotel, I wanted to whisper goodnight to my children, to crunch quietly in the snow beneath their windows and hope to hear them breathing. Yet I knew better.

I waited an interminable time at the white gates of the railway crossing. I stood dreaming of bacon and eggs and warm bread rolls for breakfast. After another train had screamed by, I shuffled over the slippery tracks and carried on past the alleyway to Hotel No6.

My eyes widened as I looked down toward the hotel courtyard to see fresh footprints in the snow. Like a bloodhound I followed them right up to the door leading to the spiral staircase. I opened it with a creak and called in.

A voice responded in the distance, a few floors up, then with the skip of shoes on stairs, Herr Ovel stood in front of me looking startled.

'Richard,' he said. 'What are you doing here?' I felt too desperate to be trivial.

'I have nowhere to stay until Christmas. I think I'm Jesus.' My humour, as it later became apparent, could not have been better placed. Herr Ovel remained surprised yet the beginnings of a grin grew across his face. Not for the first time, I had noticed a small silver cross that hung around his neck, which he now twiddled between his fingers.

After a thoughtful time he said, 'Then you better come in and I shall find space for you in the stables.'

I was, as it turned out, the only person to be staying in the hotel. Herr Ovel explained that he and his wife were about to go on a skiing holiday. With such few visitors at that time of year for a small town hotel, it was not economical to keep it open. But if I didn't mind making my own breakfast, turning the radiators back to low and dropping the keys through the post box when I left, he explained, then I could stay.

It was a generous action and I hoped that a German, in such difficulties, would receive such kindness in England. I remembered with shame the drunken anti-German songs at the football match.

I held out all of my British money, not including the money for the taxi fare. Herr Ovel graciously did not take it all and gently pulled out a couple of notes before folding the rest back into my hand. He showed me the kitchen and dangled some keys in front of me. With a small wave of his hand he left as casually as if he would be back in five minutes.

My room was situated on the first floor. It was a double room. The window that looked out onto the street had snow built up in the corner like a Christmas card. Also, it came with the added luxury of an en-suite and a television. The radiators clicked hot and my cold fingers slowly adjusted. I devoured the complimentary biscuit on the bedside cabinet before laying back on the soft smooth bed, listening to the wind outside and thinking that only moments ago I was despairing in the cold.

Chapter 25

I AWOKE THE FOLLOWING MORNING to the sound of children screaming and shrieking with joy. It was Christmas Eve and I was the only occupant of Hotel No6. My first thoughts were of my own family so I stumbled to the window in the vain hope to see their faces playing in the streets below. There was a snowball fight between young boys that drifted past the hotel. The snow had obviously fallen again throughout the night. The cobbled road was covered in a blanket of white that now had many grooves made by sledges with heavy footprints trodden in-between. Couples arm in arm shuffled happily up and down, some walking, some pulling sledges like oxen.

Everyone, as usual, wore brightly coloured hats and scarfs, mittens, and high boots. Some stopped and greeted each other, patting large gloved hands together, emitting steam from their mouths. The view from my window was a snapshot of a Christmas card, a picture of merriment. I was reminded of the cards I had often seen hanging above a fire place or standing in line along a windowsill back in England. Now I witnessed it through the window of the hotel as if I was watching it on the small television that stood in the corner of the room.

I dressed and made my way down to the kitchen. It was spotless with folded cloths hanging over the sink taps. Some large copper-bottom pots hung from hooks on the wall and a glass cabinet was full of salts and peppers, sauces and oils. I pulled out the plate of cold meats and cheeses from a large fridge that Herr Ovel had allocated for me yesterday. I found some instant tea bags in a pot on the shiny aluminium worktop. I was ravenous and had finished half of the plate before I sat down in the dining room at the table by the large thick window, which showed another angle to the Christmas card scene beyond.

It seemed that half the town was out to meet and greet each other. A brass band was playing carols off in the distance in the town square. I thought of home, I thought of my own town of Chelmsford that at that moment would also be full of people, quickly buying last minute presents or hurrying to grab a forgotten jar of pickle. Yet, here in Ahrensburg, no-one seemed to be in any kind of hurry, greeting each other as if they had recently been trapped in their houses for days by a long winter storm.

Then a sudden shock, my heart skipped a beat. Did I really see him? A little boy, his eyes barely visible below a red bobble hat, was sitting on a sledge; behind him his little sister had her hands wrapped around his waist with oversized mittens. A man I did not recognize was pulling them along. Was it really them?

My first reaction was to hit the floor: dive like Superman off a building, or like a bomb squad worker as an explosive was about to go off. Then, on the floor I thought, 'my children, my children.' I popped my head above the windowsill, squinted to focus. Without thinking I called out their names, which was impossible for anyone to hear through the thick window. The sudden sound of my voice bounced off the walls and was carried up the stairwell of the empty hotel. In an instant I was on my feet and scurrying to the door. I ran out into the snow, my skidding footprints the first markings in the flat virgin white alleyway. I was soon out on the street, sliding to a stop. Smiling people passing me on either side. I looked, I searched, but they were gone, lost in a sea of sledges, bobbled hats and fur-lined hoods. A passing couple bid me 'Fröhliche Weihnachten'. Others looked curiously at my feet; I had forgotten to put on my shoes. I headed inside, the cold already beginning to rise up to my ankles. I was soon back at the table, a trail of wet footprints following me in.

Once again I looked out at the passing people, my heart quite literally aching for my children; I wanted to hold them and not to despair.

I heard a faint ripple of applause, then the brass band continued to play. Everyone who strolled by looked happy, the brass band played carols, and children shrieked with laughter. I couldn't have felt lower. So I wept, as if I were a child myself. I wept, as I had imagined Otto weeping in the forest. I knew I looked pathetic and was relieved to have no one to pity me. An empty car park by the sea and now a solitary dining room in a deserted hotel. I couldn't pick lonelier places.

I was soon rinsing my plate and placing it in a huge but empty dishwasher in the kitchen. I headed back to my bedroom. It felt less lonesome to be within the confines of a smaller room, plus the heating was on low throughout the hotel. Although not freezing, the temperature was well below comfortable.

The radiators in my room consisted of huge bars and reminded me of the ones in my school classroom. I turned them on full and lay my damp socks on top while they clicked into heat. I had only one day to endure, just one day and my children would be mine again. I can do a day? I thought: a walk in the park, a quick stay in a hotel.

Yet alone in the room with no other thoughts to distract me I began to contemplate failure. A horrible scene of my children not being there when I arrived to collect them, or Eva's refusal to send them out. Perhaps they would not want to come: a dramatic scene, me standing alone with falling snow gathering on my shoulders.

Otto had warned me there might be problems. My heartbeat increased with the thought of failure. Surely not another flight with other people in seats originally designated for my children. It would be too much to bear. I began to feel frantic and a sudden vision of Henry in McDonald's car park came to mind. I shook the darkness from my head.

Chapter 26

SOME HOURS LATER MY EYES opened to a darkened room. It was
eerily quiet and still. I rolled off the bed and again looked out of
the window. The road outside was now completely empty. There
were the faint markings of footprints and sledge tracks still visible
under a new flurry of snow that could at least assure me that my
earlier vision had not been a dream. Yet now there was not a single
person to be seen or heard. Everyone was gone.

I took my socks from on top of the radiator; now dry; like a
warm handshake, I slid them onto my feet. I felt a sudden urge to
get out of the room. The spiral staircase was darker still. I had to
click on the timer light as I circled down to the ground floor
before opening the back door to a blast of cold arctic air. Turning
my collar up I walked out into the softly crunching snow. In the
street I peered both left and right; still not a soul to be seen, not
even a solitary person walking a dog. Everyone had already gone
somewhere. It was as if the town of Ahrensburg had been
evacuated and I had slept through it.

I decided to walk towards a different part of town as I was still
in fear of seeing my children and breaking Frau Meier's rules. As
I trudged through the centre of town, I passed the now-frozen
fountain that in summertime, people would sit around to cool off.
Beyond a slight rise was a residential area where high-rise
apartments dominated the landscape. The wind cut into my eyes

so I kept my head down and marched forward, happy to burn up energy, to burn up time.

I walked over what I believe to be a steep hill then realized when at the top and resting by a cold iron railing that I was, in fact, on a railway bridge. I looked down at two rail tracks that disappeared in a perfect line off in the distant whiteness. The snow had settled on the tracks and the wires above hung heavy with icicles.

I felt perplexed and couldn't understand why a town so recently full of life and laughter could so quickly become devoid of people. I was beginning to take it personally.

After my slow descent off the bridge I turned onto a path that snaked in-between some large apartment blocks the size of multi-storey car parks.

The many apartments were of the usual German construction, in that each one had a huge front room window almost full length from floor to ceiling that looked out onto the world. There were no net curtains to obscure their views. My solitary figure trudging through the snow must have been the only moving focal point from within these warm apartments.

I first noticed a little boy of about six or seven with his hands pressed against the glass staring down at me from four floors up. I stopped and stared back and wondered whether he could see me smile. He beckoned to someone behind him before another boy, a little older, joined him at the window. Then, to his left a few floors down, another child begun to stare out of the window at me too, then another a few windows away and another and another until the windows on many different floors began to fill with little faces staring, wide eyed, down at me.

I blew on my hands, and stamped my feet but did not move on. The longer I stayed there the more children came to other windows, some accompanied by adults, others with siblings holding toys in their hands. Over a quarter of the windows in my view had someone looking down at me.

One child appeared holding a piece of torn wrapping paper and it struck me in an instant as I recalled why everyone had disappeared from the streets: In Germany in late afternoon on the twenty-fourth of December, Christmas presents are handed out. I realised now that everyone had gone home to celebrate Christmas and in Germany, everyone means everyone.

So now I had a better idea as to why these children were so curious to see somebody outside. Each apartment window resembled a box in a theatre and I was on stage; a lone cold actor; Shakespeare in the snow. There was a strange sense of power in that they could all only see me but I alone could see all of them.

I gave a small gentle wave of my hand and in return received the overwhelming compassion of fifty German children, all unaware of each other. I felt like they were telling me not to give up on my own family, willing me to take them home because before I could put my cold hand back into my pocket, every single staring child, in every single window was waving back.

*

I RETURNED TO FIND THE hotel looking hauntingly dark with only my bedroom light to show an inhabitancy. The streetlights flickered on and illuminated the snowflakes that floated by like lazy white moths. I had arrived back outside the Hotel via a different direction and recognized my own solitary footprints from where I had set of in the other direction, now slightly covered by snow flurries. It was a reminder, as if I needed one, that I was truly the only one outside.

The large back door of the hotel creaked open to a still and dark interior with dim outlines of unfamiliar furniture. I clicked on the timer light and headed swiftly up the spiral stairs to my room, shutting the bedroom door on the cold hotel outside.

I drew the curtains, warmed my hands on the radiator and switched on the small television. The screen flickered, before the serious face of a newsreader appeared speaking sternly in sharp, precise rolling German. The backdrop to the presenter was of a car that had skidded off an icy road. I automatically listened, forgetting for a moment that I couldn't understand. I turned the dial to another channel. This time the scene was an aerial shot from high inside a cathedral, where the miniature choir boys were singing while a priest or vicar, I could never tell which, walked in between the aisles swinging a smoking vase like a beekeeper.

I clicked the dial again and to my surprise and immediate comfort I heard English voices. It was an old black and white film, set around 1920s England. It was of a butler who, while serving drinks to his master would sneak one drink for himself. The butler got drunker and drunker yet still managed, somewhat acrobatically to arrive at the table with drinks. I giggled to myself, then laughed out-loud, laying on the bed as if I were at home. When the programme finished it was swiftly followed by an advert of an expressionless man standing outside of a car show room. I switched the television off and the silence was intimidating.

The walk had exhausted me so I set the travel alarm clock I had brought from England before curling up on the bed. I felt proud and relieved that I had made it to the end of another day in Germany without my children. It was difficult to rest at first as I thought of all the waving hands and tiny faces in the apartment windows. Or perhaps I was like every other child back in England on Christmas Eve; too excited to sleep.

Chapter 27

I DID NOT SLEEP, INSTEAD merely drifted in and out of semi consciousness. Occasionally I would sit up with a start and quickly reach over to my travel alarm clock and check the time.

Eventually I got up, stretched and opened the curtains. It remained dark outside. My alarm clock glowed six-forty am. I still had four hours to my precise pick-up time of 10am. There was nothing to pack and nothing to do except clean my room and leave a note of thanks on the pillow.

In two days I had barely spoken to a single person. I could last a few more hours, I thought. So I lay back on the bed and closed my eyes to replay again the smooth version of my children running into my arms; Eva happily waving us off as our taxi drove away.

I awoke again some hours later and stretched for the alarm clock: 8.47am. I had just over an hour to go; time was moving on and my excitement and apprehension began to build.

Once dressed, I strolled lazily down the stairs to the kitchen in search of some food and stared hopefully into the large fridge. I took out one of the small pots of jam, which normally was placed on each table and jumped up onto the cold aluminium worktop to eat, my legs swinging like a child. I dipped my finger into the jam; it tasted too sweet and I clicked my tongue as if I'd sucked a lemon.

Then, as I looked up to the wall, my heart skipped a beat. In the shock I bit my finger. I quickly put the jam pot down and ran up the stairs, diving into my bedroom, grabbing the alarm clock. I read the dial aloud and screamed. The clock I had seen on the kitchen wall was one hour in advance of my alarm clock, which, I had forgotten, my God, I had forgotten, to set forward one hour to German time. I now had merely ten minutes to present myself at the back door of the tobacconist shop.

I scurried around the room at full speed, flinging the covers over the bed, squeezing the last remaining things into my bag. There was no time for a shower; there was no time to comb my hair. I skipped down the spiral staircase and locked the door behind me and shoved the key back through the slot.

I had one job, I thought, one thing in two days of waiting and I might be late. Scurrying like a hamster, slipping and sliding in the snow, I came to a skidding stop outside of the shop. I pulled out the small alarm clock; I had made it with three minutes to spare.

I took a moment to catch my breath, leaning against the cold glass of the shop window. I must not, I reminded myself, be smug or provocative, moody or sharp, or to engage in a conversation that might lead to an argument; better still, not to engage in any conversation at all. I must not mention the empty hotel I had stayed in or the long travel from England, the ferries and the plane flights; the endless hours of loneliness and despair; the injustice and rage at a rigged system. Don't mention the pain, and shame of crying myself to sleep; of their empty bedrooms with cupboards full of clothes discarded like unwanted orphans. Don't talk about money, begging from friends, the humiliation of taking a wad of cash from my mother's gently trembling hand. And for God's sake whatever I did, I must not talk about the wicked witch of the North: her mother. I must mention nothing of the things that led up to me now waiting outside in the snow.

Above all, I willed myself to be brave and not to ask about the man I'd seen pulling the sledge. Just collect your children, I promised myself with a smile, and get to the airport and leave like a gust of wind.

I faced the back door, rapidly sucking in the air to regulate my breathing. Then in an action rehearsed many times I reached out and knocked. In the silence that followed the colour drained from my face with each second of uncertainty that passed.

I heard an excited child's scream…. my child; it was followed by sound of wooden clogs clapping on the steps that led down the worn marble staircase. Eva opened the door.

She was wearing a white roll-neck jumper that came up to her chin and look down at me from the elevated doorway with her piercing grey-blue eyes.

'You look awful and you are a few minutes early,' she said then closed the door again.

I did not move a muscle and stood rooted to the spot as if my feet were frozen to the ground, which, in fact, they were beginning to do.

I listened intently to the muffled sounds of what I presumed were hurried preparations: coats being put on, zips pulled up, passports checked. I waited in nervous tension for the expectant speech to accompany the hand over, a telling-off; a list of rules of what and what not to do; the finger wagging warnings.

Moments later Eva opened the door and the children pushing by her legs to run to me. I knelt down in the snow and wrapped my arms around them, their warm cheeks smooshed against mine. I sighed aloud.

'Oh I've missed you, I've missed you so much.'

As I slowly stood up again I scanned Eva from bottom to top. I started with her clogs that had just clanged down the stairs, up the length of her red jogging bottoms to the frayed edged of the shaggy woollen white roll neck jumper before seeing the straight cut ends of her hair; then passing her uncovered lips and nose that was reddened by the cold. I stared into her eyes and just for a moment we were alone.

Her hair was silky; she had obviously just combed it, perhaps for me and I took strength from the thought. I felt sure she was going to smile yet her expression, however forced remained cold. She quickly looked away. I couldn't place her emotion; it was not in line with the situation. Something was up.

I was expecting Eva and the children to have a teary goodbye; perhaps they had already done this upstairs when they had heard the knock at the door. At the request of Eva both the children spun around to show me their matching backpacks.

'You still have some clothes in England so I've just packed for carry-on luggage,' she said then added somewhat tentatively, 'I've packed the children's passports too.'

I shot her a glare at the mention of passports that would now be German. She quickly retreated while bidding the children goodbye. There were no tears as she began to close the door. Perhaps she was down-grading the emotions of the situation so as not to upset the children who were unfazed and stood looking at me with red noses. It was all too quick.

'Eva,' I shouted although I was lost of what to say next. She held the door ajar with only a slice of her face on show.

'What do you want?'

I searched for something to say but all I could think of was, 'Merry Christmas.'

The door clicked shut. *Merry Christmas*, I sneered to myself. What was I thinking?

I turned to hug the children who were waiting expectantly, their trusting eyes peering out from within their hoods. Then after I had zipped up their coats I heard the sound of Eva's clogs going up the stairs. She had remained for some moments on the other side of the closed door.

I grabbed my children's hands and hurried to the front of the shop. The yellow Mercedes, with its exhaust rhythmically puffing was waiting, the large animated face of my friendly taxi driver smiling from within; I blessed the reliability of German time keeping.

I recognised the clicking sound of the boot releasing and I heaved my bag and the children's little back packs into the boot, then I lifted both Sebastian and Louise into the back seats. As I drew closer to buckle them in, their little faces nestled into mine and they giggled. It was as if we had never been parted.

As the taxi pulled away I looked up to the apartment window in a vain hope that Eva would be looking out. She was not.

Chapter 28

THE ROADS TO THE AIRPORT had been cleared of snow, which was banked up on either side, resembling a long white corridor. Yet the brisk wind that came in sudden bursts often swept the snow over the road again making our progress painfully slow. I spent a nervous hour looking at the wristwatch of the taxi driver as well as the meter while giving reassuring smiles to the children. I wished that the arrangements laid down by the German court had given allowances for delays. We were going to be late and with every snowdrift that spilled onto the road, the taxi reduced its speed and my anxiety grew.

Eventually, beyond a snow covered roundabout, I noticed the large, brightly lit, green house structure of the airport terminal. Surrounded by white, it resembled an ice castle.

The taxi driver was able to pull up directly outside of the glass frontage due to the lack of other traffic. It looked empty inside. Only one airline desk had its lights on and a single staff member stood behind the counter.

A solitary cleaner pushed a trolley full of brooms, hops and a half-filled rubbish bags across the vast, shiny white floor. The taxi driver again refused to take a tip and instead produced a bag of liquorice from under his seat that he had obviously saved for Sebastian and Louise. As I unbuckled my seat belt he leaned towards me and ruffled my hair, saying something in German and

I believe, in that precise moment, we both remembered the time before when I had cried in his taxi.

The cold air was crisp and bracing. After I had helped my children out of their seats, we stepped outside onto the pavement. They became excited at seeing the large Christmas tree inside the terminal and were soon pushing through the revolving doors ahead of me. I did not know whether they were happy to be going on holiday or if, like me, they were eager to leave Germany before they could be stopped. Every step, I thought, was a step nearer to home.

Inside the terminal I passed an air stewardess who was on her way out. She forced her last smile of the day and directed us to the one remaining check-in desk that was still in operation. I looked up at the flight information board: my flight from Hamburg to Gatwick was the last one showing as outbound and to my alarm was now boarding.

Another young stewardess with heavy make-up hurriedly glanced at my tickets and to my relief said that we could take our bags as carry-on. I offered my passport but instead she pointed towards a single passport booth that had been hastily set up at the far end of the terminal where the last passengers waited patiently in a line.

We truly are the last people to fly today, I thought, and as if to confirm this, no sooner had I taken the children's hands and walked towards passport control, the lights of the last working desk flickered off. I turned to see the desk clerk sling a handbag over her shoulder.

I guided the children over to a seat near passport control and began to rummage through their backpacks. Louise was beginning to get restless and elbowed Sebastian who responded in kind, their insults half in German. I pulled them apart. I didn't want to be sharp with them, not now, not in the airport, so calmed them as best I could with whispered rebukes and bribes of liquorice.

I began to search, first into Sebastian's bag and then Louise's bag for the passports. I could not find them. I checked the pockets of the children's coats and again the bags. Still nothing.

I searched again, this time more studiously, emptying the contents onto the floor. A hard plastic dinosaur smacked onto the ground. I looked over to the lone customs-officer who sat in his portable booth reading a magazine. He looked up momentarily then went back to his reading.

Again I checked their coat pockets and every sleeve and zipped compartment of their bags. I made the children stand up and I felt around their person and shook their bags upside down so that all the little bits of dust and sweets wrappers and pencil shavings came fluttering out.

'Where are your passports?' I said holding mine up in full view. The children looked bemused and clearly did not know what I was asking.

It hit me in a horrible wave. I recalled Eva's reluctance for conversation, her guilty, evasive facial expression, her averted gaze, and eagerness to be gone. I had seen it but not fully comprehended. Of course, that was why she had not said goodbye to the children; she had not packed their passports so she knew they would be coming back.

I looked around in despair. The waiting line of passengers on the other side of the barrier was now slowly filtering through a door marked boarding; they were going to the promise land; escaped prisoners on the other side of the wire. There was no time to travel back to Ahrensburg to collect the passports.

I closed my eyes, squeezing my lids together, hoping all would be good when I opened them. Both of my children read the seriousness on my face and looked to me for comfort. I forced a smile, which never reached my eyes; my dreams of Christmas with my children in England scattered across the floor like the contents of their backpacks.

I had been beaten; fallen at the last hurdle. Otto had warned me of this. The judge would never believe it: the misplaced passports would be explained away and I, the muddled English father, always arriving late, couldn't even be trusted to organise his own children's journey back to England. Perhaps they would think I had never wanted to go anyway, just one of those fathers who liked to argue for the sake of it.

Both of the children, without being asked, hopped off their seats and began to quietly help me put their things back into their bags. It was a pitiful scene.

Then, while holding my passport, I remembered. I quickly flicked through the pages until I found the one with my children's names printed on it. A long shot I thought, as I was well aware that British law had only recently introduced the requirement, in line with Germany, that children must travel with their own passports. But this was Germany and although they too required their children to have their own passports, did the customer's officer know that this law now extended to England?

I looked over to the booth. The officer was young with pale white skin that had not seen the sunshine; there were a few acne spots around his chin. It was probably his youth and unmarried status that ensured his allocation for the Christmas Eve shift.

'Now listen to me,' I said in a stern whisper. 'You have got to be really good and not cry or argue.' I pointed surreptitiously at the passport booth. 'We are going to walk past that man. Do not speak to him unless he speaks to you and whatever you do, do…not…speak…in…German.' They received my request in long-faced silence.

I harnessed the children with their little backpacks, Sebastian insisting on holding his dinosaur in his hand. We marched the long walk to the passport booth, a mere thirty paces in actual distance but a lifetime with each step in slow motion. I did not know whether to smile or frown, to look hurried or casual.

The customs officer put down his magazine and folded it away in his jacket pocket. I rather hoped he was making ready to leave. Close up, he appeared even younger in his crisp brown shirt and official cap that seemed too large for his head. I hesitated to walk straight up to the small counter and stopped a metre off at the line on the floor and waited for him to beckon me forward; make him feel important, I thought.

I handed over my passport then quickly looked down at Louise pretending to pander to a need and zipped up her coat. There was a moment when Louise went to speak and I quickly stared her down. I waited in reverent silence for the officer to finish leafing through my passport. He glanced at me and then back at my passport.

'Und die Kinder?' he asked. I quickly lifted Louise onto my hip to distract her from speaking. I casually motioned with my finger for the custom officer to turn the page. He did so and I watched his eyes as they scanned the names of my children. I offered to show him my flight tickets as another distraction, which he waved away.

Then in an instant, he clapped my passport shut and handed it back. I thanked him in English and began to walk through. Within a few metres of passing, the light in the booth was switched off.

We joined the end of the moving queue. The stewardess tore the stubs of our tickets and her eyes, surrounded by blue mascara, barely glanced at my passport. The children ran ahead down the suspended corridor to the aircraft, which wobbled slightly with the motion. We took a row of three seats with me sitting in the middle.

I coupled both of them in my arms as we watched a steward pull and lock the aircraft door. Louise looked up to me. 'I didn't speak in German' she said.

At home in England I imagined a waiting brass band, conductor poised with his baton ready to start the music as soon as we walked through the arrivals door. Glitter, confetti and balloons would drop from the ceiling, a little girl in a ball gown would run up and present us with flowers; petals strewn at our feet. We had made it.

Yet a different home awaited me now. The poet Wordsworth was right in that. I had a few precious days to be a father again, to get close to my children and them to me. I could at last step out of the shadows.

I was proud and wanted to show the whole of England that I had my children again. Yet estranged fathers who knew my situation avoided me, and only if cornered would assuage their guilt by offering the reasons why they had given up on their own family. They held their manhood cheap. Mothers too could be evasive; those who had been through the divorce system viewed me as the enemy. Prams were pushed to the other side of the road.

My world was different now, where my kids, Dave, Frau Meier, Frau and Herr Ovel, and Otto were the only people that mattered. When I opened the front door to my house, my children ran up the stairs to their bedrooms as if they had never left. That evening I popped my head around the door to watch them gently sleeping.

In that moment it seemed inconceivable that I would ever take them back to Germany. Yet in the recesses of my mind I knew that we would return, back to the system that had held onto them so vigorously. However, Germany was no longer a foreign land, and me a foreigner in it. I had a home to stay in, albeit a hotel bedroom, and familiar faces to greet me. Most of all, I knew that when I eventually walked back through the arrivals lounge, holding two tired children by the hand, I could look for the man with a shiny head who would hold his arms out to welcome me. I was not alone, and would never again step into the shadows.

THE END

Other novels, novellas and short story collections available from Stairwell Books

Blackbird's Song	Katy Turton
Eboracvm the Fortess	Graham Clews
The Warder	Susie Williamson
The Great Billy Butlin Race	Robin Richards
Mistress	Lorraine White
Life Lessons by Libby	Libby and Laura Engel-Sahr
Waters of Time	Pauline Kirk
Waiting at the Temporary Traffic Lights	Graham Lee
The Tao of Revolution	Chris Taylor
The Water Bailiff's Daughter	Yvonne Hendrie
O Man of Clay	Eliza Mood
Eboracvm: the Village	Graham Clews
Sammy Blue Eyes	Frank Beill
Margaret Clitherow	John and Wendy Rayne-Davis
Serpent Child	Pat Riley
Rocket Boy	John Wheatcroft
Virginia	Alan Smith
Looking for Githa	Patricia Riley
On Suicide Bridge	Tom Dixon
Something I Need to Tell You	William Thirsk-Gaskill
Poetic Justice	P J Quinn
Return of the Mantra	Susie Williamson
The Martyrdoms at Clifford's Tower 1190 and 1537	John Rayne-Davis
The Go-To Guy	Neal Hardin
Abernathy	Claire Patel-Campbell
Tyrants Rex	Clint Wastling
A Shadow in My Life	Rita Jerram
Rapeseed	Alwyn Marriage
Thinking of You Always	Lewis Hill
Know Thyself	Lance Clarke
How to be a Man	Alan Smith
Here in the Cull Valley	John Wheatcroft
Tales from a Prairie Journal	Rita Jerram
Border 7	Pauline Kirk
Homelands	Shaunna Harper
49	Paul Lingaard
The Geology of Desire	Clint Wastling
When the Crow Cries	Maxine Ridge
Close Disharmony	P J Quinn
Poison Pen	P J Quinn

For further information please contact rose@stairwellbooks.com

www.stairwellbooks.co.uk
@stairwellbooks

CPSIA information can be obtained
at www.ICGtesting.com
Printed in the USA
BVHW081323211021
619527BV00007B/65